CAVIARE

CAVIARE

a novel by

Godfrey Smith

HODDER AND STOUGHTON
LONDON SYDNEY AUCKLAND TORONTO

The extracts from 'Time was away' and 'The Eclogue for Christmas' by Louis MacNeice from *The Collected Poems of Louis MacNeice* are reproduced by permission of Faber and Faber Ltd.

For
Alexandra, Emily, Rayne, Robin and Tom with love.

Time was away and somewhere else.
There were two glasses and two chairs
And two people with the one pulse
(Somebody stopped the moving stairs) :
Time was away and somewhere else.

LOUIS MACNEICE

1 Don't laugh: but for me New York was once an
enchanted city. That was some twenty years ago when
you could still arrive year round by ocean liner. Those
days Manhattan island came out of the light mist on that fifth
morning as you surfaced early to get your hangover freshly
laundered by the minted sea breeze and your body braced by
the cold smash of the ship's pool. Those days, they had a breakfast menu that would have done for the Duponts or Rockefellers
and I suppose some staunch souls went through it finnan
haddies and all. I was always happy with some scrambled eggs
and newly milled coffee. It was a time when America was still a
huge word, a magnificent idea, a stretching of the senses, a backdrop against which the impossible could be played out. It was
the place where at last those with a termagant spirit gnawing
them to do a new thing, essay some great leap of the imagination, some enormous bound of the faculties, could make it, try
it, do it. It was Arcadia fashioned in concrete; the only proper
target for all occidental ambitions; it was the factory where
myths were wrought and dreams hammered into practical
shapes.

The city seemed to float then a bit, as if scooped out of air and
light; and indeed if you think about it you might agree that
those few very great human constructions that eventually matter
have this insubstantial quality; though made as functional office
towers or boring apartment blocks they are pleasure domes to
the mind's eye. The first time I saw Manhattan, from the deck
of *Queen Elizabeth I*, it seemed to ride gently on the early morning sunlight, and the Hudson River which we now desecrate as
a monumental cesspool, seemed to sparkle with the promise of
delights soon to come ashore. Poor deluded Limey that I was;
and yet, for a little while, there was a kind of magic there, as I
shall try to relate.

The last time I was there, though, just last November, the promise had long melted away. The city had become an unsmiling hinterland which one visited only to wrest a tribute; and/or to squeeze it of almighty dollars while there was still time. It was no place to visit for fun. I was there strictly on business.

Most Englishmen make for the Algonquin if they can; some idiot American professor once talked me into staying at the New York Hilton because, he averred, the view from the forty-second floor was so majestic; and so maybe it was for the five minutes you wanted to take it in; otherwise it was nowheresville; a billion dollar nightmare. I've seldom felt so threatened or so empty anywhere. So this time I beat it back to the Algonquin which, for all its faults, is still peopled with human beings.

Because I needed time to prepare, I flew in this time on Friday; the lunchtime Jumbo from London lands you up at the hotel round six their time, eleven hours, and the only sensible thing to do is head for an early bed and let the natural juices smooth you out as you sleep; this was my invariable plan. I had no appointments till Monday and no social engagements till then. It's odd how New Yorkers, the most hospitable of people, make the lemming rush for the country on Friday and sometimes unwittingly leave their visitors behind to fend for themselves; I don't complain about this because they make up for it all right the other five days of the week. But they often assume you're with someone else for the weekend; and though sometimes you are, sometimes you aren't, and so this sixty-six hour gap suddenly opens up in front of you. It may be — it certainly was in my case — the longest time you've ever spent in the company of no other human being you know, and this is a good therapy, a little like going on a forty-eight hour fast say, to cleanse the system whether of material or psychic sediment. So I didn't mind the thought of that hole between then and now.

Yet when I got to the reception desk at the Algonquin, I discovered that at any rate three human beings in the city knew and cared that I was there. The hotel clerk handed me two envelopes and a small packet. I think I had some curious premonition about the packet, which was only some two inches square by half an inch deep, and I left it to the last. I sat down on my bed, my bags still unpacked, and tried the two letters.

2

The first was marked Private and Confidential. Inside, the address was deceptively simple, and the message that followed mpler still:

> Bureau of Internal Security,
> Washington DC.

Dear Mr. Freeman,

I should be obliged if you could spare me a little time on Saturday. There is a matter of some delicacy and importance in which you may be able to help us. If you will let me know a convenient moment I will call at the hotel.

> Faithfully,
> Edward B. Scrutton
> (Admiral US Navy retd.)

I was not all that surprised. I'm an interpreter by trade, and though we're international civil servants we just occasionally get a light arm laid on us by the security people. The only practical answer to all such overtures is nuts: your total neutrality is the badge of your office. At the U.N. we're called the fifth wall. But of course we sometimes hear things that could be useful, hence the try-on. I dialled the admiral's number at Washington and told his answering service I'd be delighted to meet him at ten. That's late for an American appointment, but I can't think clearly much before then.

The second missive was in a familiar hand:

> NYC Thurs

Dearest Ben,

How lovely that you're back in town and how hateful of you as usual not to let me know. I'm scribbling this now Ben because you must be careful; it's the old problem back again only this time it could be much more dangerous. Ben I worry about you because you're such an innocent. The security people here are very tough and you could get hurt. So do please take my advice. For heaven's sake talk to them all you know and get them out of your hair. Which day shall we have lunch? Monday would suit me best say 12 noon at the Algonquin.

> All love,
> Sue.

This mixture of unpunctuated concern and loving exhortation rang, as always, like some temporarily distanced wife keeping her finger on me. Sue was not exactly that but she was an old friend who cared. She was doing a spell in New York with her husband who was in our delegation at the United Nations. She was not given to histrionics and I felt a vague sense of unease at her warning. I turned to the little packet. It contained a royal blue box embossed with an ornate gold coat of arms. Inside there lay a curious gold ring, or more precisely, a section of one. It was oval, and intricately chased. It was so made that it would fit together with six other segments to make one exceedingly beautiful signet. It was about two hundred years old and was, to my knowledge, unique in the entire craft of jewellery. It had once been owned by the Russian royal family, who had given it away for services rendered to them. It took hours to fit together: I could never do it. But I knew someone who could:

Ben my darling, (ran the note inside the box) this is just to prove that it's really me. What a sweet joke of the goddess to throw us together in this place at this time. I've so much to tell you. But I'm watched always. There's a little boat that goes round Manhattan on tourist trips. We could talk there. It's the Circle Line. Pier 83. Three p.m. Sunday. I'm longing to see you. — L.

I picked up the sliver of curving gold that had been lovingly fashioned by some Persian craftsman two centuries ago. The Russians called it the Enigma Ring, and you could find footnotes about it in their history books. It was supposed to bring luck to the wearer but death if you lost it, and all that crap. I had owned it once. The only person I knew who could put it together was the girl who had once given it to me, the one who had written the note inviting me to Pier 83 the next day. Her name was Leila, and she was the lost love of my young days.

2 The Admiral was punctual. He had the booze-ruddy face and slightly stoned blue eyes of someone who's been at sea overlong. He looked rather too honest for the job.

'Good morning, Admiral.'

'Good morning, sir.' He said 'sir' American style, as the French say monsieur; a mark of respect between equals, all men being, for the sake of the game, equals.

'How about some coffee — or maybe a drink?'

'No thank you, sir. May we talk in your room?'

'I'd rather we took a walk.'

Obviously my room was already bugged, but the streets of Manhattan were not. Or then again maybe they were.

'As you wish.'

'Tell you what; let's go down-town. I've always meant to do my duty and walk round historic New York, but never had the time.'

'By all means.'

We took a taxi and sped south to Bowling Green, the place where Peter Minuit is said to have bought Manhattan island from the Indians for twenty-four dollarsworth of trinkets. It was football weather and the morning sun sluiced down between the gaunt grey canyons in great bucketsful of liquid gold. It was hardly possible to compass in words; an anthem in steel and glass to so much power, so much greed, so much glory, so much graft. When I catch the city in that mood, I never know whether to laugh or cry.

We strolled down Whitehall Street, and up Pearl Street to Fraunces Tavern. Only it isn't the original building, but just a skilful reconstruction of the house where Washington said farewell to his officers after the Revolution. Good it is, great it isn't. There's a museum of revolutionary relics inside, but we decided to skip that. The Admiral cleared his throat.

5

'May I ask you, sir, if you know a lady called Leila Haven?'

'Yes I do. She's not a lady, incidentally.'

'You know her well?'

'I used to. Why? You're from the CIA, I suppose?'

'No sir. Not the CIA. I am not their responsibility. I am responsible only to one man.'

'I see.'

'Yes sir. Now I am deeply interested in the case of Miss Leila Haven.'

'So am I.'

'Many people are deeply interested in Miss Haven.'

'I can only answer for myself.'

'Of course, sir. Now, would you be so kind as to tell me one or two things about her? You see, she is of very unusual interest to my country.'

'What about my country?'

'They too are interested.'

'Everybody is interested.'

'Yes.'

'What do you want to know?'

'A few simple questions.'

'What sort of questions?'

He turned and considered me, his vein-mottled face bricked up with care.

'How long have you known Miss Haven?'

'A long time.'

'May I ask how you met?'

'Socially.'

'She was a good friend of yours?'

'How do you mean, was?'

'She still is?'

'Yes.'

'Would you describe her as intelligent?'

'Yes. In some ways. In other ways she was a prodigious twerp.'

The Admiral paused in his steps and looked to make sure I wasn't kidding.

'Excuse me sir. A prodigious — '

'Twerp. Moron. Idiot.'

'You did say — was?'

'Yes. She was a twerp.'

6

'Not new?'

'She may have learned a bit of sense.'

'You still feel a particular affection for Miss Haven?'

'I adore her.'

'Ah.'

We walked along in silence, turned past Delmonico's and crossed Broad Street where the old Dutch canal used to run. The Admiral seemed to be struggling over the next bit.

'I believe you are married, sir.'

'That's right.'

Another of those intermissions. This time I decided to serve first.

'I knew Leila long before I was married. We met when we were children.'

He didn't sound very interested; but then he would have known already.

'Now, sir, if I may ask you this — and I'm sorry to say it is relevant — did Miss Haven ever discuss politics with you?'

'Not much. She was something of a determinist, so there wasn't a good deal to discuss.'

We paused and faced each other. Above us towered No. 1 Broadway, the place where they say, God save us, the first martini was made.

'Did she ever talk about the United States?'

'Not much. Even then, only specifics. Small silly things about America which delighted or irritated her.' We began to head up Broadway.

'Do you know Mr. Charles Harbinger?'

'Yes. We met at Oxford.'

Now we were getting somewhere.

'Do you still keep in touch with Mr Harbinger?'

'Off and on. He looks me up when he has time passing through London. And I'm on his mailing list. Every time he makes one of those great, turgid boring speeches of his he sends me a copy.'

The Admiral looked shocked. This was no way to speak of the President's favourite adviser. It's one of the weird consequences, incidentally, of having been at Oxford in that hallucinatory spell just after the war, that you can't help knowing a whole clutch of people who are now world names: Presidents and Prime Ministers of emergent countries whom you remember only because they were always pissed in the afternoon, though forbidden alcohol by their religion; and even the Rhodes Scholars had naturally enough done pretty well. Charles was a tall, loosely articulated New Englander who had an engineering degree from MIT and had already been through Harvard Business School. He took a PhD in politics at Oxford, joined the Grid-iron which is the aristo's dining club, got his grey flannel suits from the Prince of Wales's old tailors in the High Street, and rowed number six for the university. He had straw-coloured hair and slightly bulging light blue eyes — he was from an old Dutch family — and he always seemed to twitch slightly. He was charming and polite and fearfully rich. He could afford an MG, which most undergraduates couldn't in those days, and even then he used to give working breakfasts to discuss life, liberty, and the pursuit of happiness. It was fairly obvious that he was going far.

The Admiral permitted himself a quick smile. I wondered if Charles knew about this conversation. Evidently he wasn't supposed to know.

'Do I take it, sir, that you and Mr. Harbinger don't see eye to eye?'

'Not at all. We're buddies. If you can only get him off politics he's very good company. A credit to you.'

'And was it you who introduced Miss Haven to Mr. Harbinger?'

I had realised for some time that this was coming.

'I thought you knew the answers to all these questions already.'

'We know most of them, sir. But we have to check and re-check.'

'Yes. I introduced them.'

'They became friendly quickly?'

'Yes. I believe he propositioned her the first evening.'

The Admiral stared at the pavement as if he were seeking a good spot to throw up.

'I shouldn't have said that. I'm joking of course.'

He was still looking.

'What do you think was the attraction, sir?'

'You mean what did she see in him?'

'Firstly, yes.'

'Innocence.'

'And — '

8

'And what did she have to offer him in return?'
'Yes.'
I thought this one over.
'The luxury of doubt.'
'That's very interesting.'
'It's precisely what it was all about.'
He stopped and faced me.
'I'm sure you will appreciate that this is not a very pleasant duty for me.'
'Yes, I can see that.'
'Do you — does Mr. Harbinger strike you as a stable person?'
'Frankly, no.'
'Have you any concrete evidence for saying that?'
'I should have thought you have far more information on that score than I do.'
'We are interested in what you have to say.'
We had got to Wall Street. It was my turn to halt.
'I'm talking a good deal without having too clear an idea what this is all about. I realise that it's important to the United States government. I don't want to be obstructive. But anything I can tell you is bound to be trivial. I said I'd see you because I thought it would help her. And him, for that matter. Now I'm beginning to wonder.'
'You must realise, sir, that we have to build up quite an intricate mosaic of information.'
'I know, Admiral. Mountains and mountains of brute fact.'
'It has to be done.'
'Tell me how serious it is.'
'As you yourself said, sir, anything to do with Mr. Charles Harbinger is a serious matter for my government.'
'But what harm can she possibly do now?'
'None, now. We can look after the future.'
'You're surely not concerned about the past?'
'There are still some facts we should like to know.'
'I don't think you need any more facts. I think you need less. What you want is not facts but ideas. You want to take a view about her. You have to try and decide how much harm she's done.'
'Or might do.'
'You said you could look after the future.'
'Once we know how to deal with it.'

9

'Why can't you be more explicit?'

'Why can't you?'

Now the preliminary courtesies were over, we seemed almost to like each other.

'Look, Admiral, I think I want to help you. I like to think the truth will help them both. I could talk to you about Leila all night if I could be sure of that. But when I'd be finished, would you really be any the wiser?'

'I might be. Let me put it this way, sir. We should greatly appreciate your help in alleviating our concern.'

'That's what I hoped you'd say.'

He produced a card.

'Would you think systematically over everything you can remember about Miss Haven, and then call me at this number?'

'All right. I'll see what I can remember. But I'm not too hopeful.' I paused. 'One thing though I can tell you now. I'd trust her anywhere.'

He looked genuinely puzzled.

'You would trust her?'

'Yes. Anywhere. Any time.'

He gave me one last look, this mottled sailor carrying a great imagined burden on his square shoulders.

'Thank you, Mr. Freeman. You have been very co-operative.'

He shook hands and hailed a taxi.

'Would you like a lift?'

'No thanks, I'd like to walk north a few blocks and think.'

'Very well, sir. Goodbye.'

I was alone at the point where the old city of New Amsterdam had once ended in a giant stockade to hold back the Indians; that wall which had given its name to the richest street in the world. I felt relatively pleased at the way things had gone. One thing was certain: by my final words I had made tolerably certain of being ruled out of the case: anyone who trusted Leila was by definition zonked out of his skull. That was neat. On the other hand, I was now quite certain that she was in bad trouble.

3   Back at the Algonquin the noon drinkers were
    beginning to arrive; mainly social topers with just the
    odd hard case siphoned off into the Blue Bar. The
little newsagent in the corner of the room was doing a good
trade in *New York Magazine* and even the *New York Review of
Books*, for this was still the heartland of the city's radical chic
establishment. The men looked groomed and confident: flat
stomachs, carefully nourished on proteins and salads, tucked
into five hundred dollar suits. They greeted each other with
honest-to-god sounds and tribal greeting gestures: Well Mel —
hug, slap, shake — it's so *good to see you*. They were like a new
race of Romans: rulers, engineers, soldiers; they were bridge-
builders and empire-makers. At least that's how they seemed
that morning in the Algonquin. The thunder of their plumbing
and the swish of their icy showers when they rose punctually at
six each day in the rooms adjacent to mine in the hotel were
impressive in their strength of purpose; and the energy of their
copulation each night — the walls were pretty thin — quite
awe-inspiring. The women looked good too with their trochaic
voices and freshly brushed hair and Gucci bags and legs
divinely turned on God's lathe. Of course, you can find jerks
and broads by the quarter million in this city as in any other;
only they weren't there that morning. I sat in one of the armchairs and pinged my bell for the waiter. I ordered a gin and
tonic with plenty of limes since we can't or don't get them in
Limeyland and I let all the expensively produced people melt
into one well-bred, well-heeled blur while I remembered the
time I thought Leila was dead.

4 I thought Leila was dead one chill January morning when the sky was the colour of that off-white Harrods writing paper and the stone tiles on the six hundred year old roofs of our village glistened in the rain like freshly-caught mackerel. Not her sort of day; yet since I had in a sense been expecting the news for a good many years the sadness was contained. I had made the emotional box to put it in long ago. One of the consolations of being over forty is that bad news is seldom as bad as good news is good. We know there is going to be plenty of bad news this decade and the good, when it comes, is so unexpected. Still, it would be vain to pretend that the news failed to hurt. Though I'd written Leila down in my balance sheet each year, her going still diminished me.

The man at *The Times* told me. They still break bad news very well there.

'Is that Mr. Benjamin Freeman?'

'Yes.'

'Oh, good morning, Mr. Freeman. This is *The Times* newspaper.'

'Good morning.'

'I'm afraid we have bad news of an old friend of yours.'

The discounting system did its swift work and I was half ready when he went on:

'It's Leila Haven. We have a report that she is dead.'

Yet not ready enough.

'How do you mean, a report? There've been so many speculations.'

'It's true, I fear. Our own people have already confirmed it.'

'I see.'

'May we offer you our sympathy? I believe you knew her well.'

'Yes, I did know her. Do you want me to bring that thing up to date?'

'We should be most grateful. It's most interesting, but it is of course some ten or twelve years since you wrote it.'

'Is it because of the work she's done or the other business?'

A well-bred pause. Then: 'Both are of course, important.'

'I'll do what I can. There's not a lot of reliable information.'

'Yes, we appreciate that. However, clearly we must do what we can to complete the story.'

'I'll do my best. Will you send me round a copy? I don't think I still have it.'

'Certainly. By hand. If you could compress the new matter into, say, 300 words?'

'I doubt if there's that much to say.'

'We leave it in your good hands, Mr. Freeman. She seems to have been quite a remarkable lady.'

'She wasn't a lady.'

'May we have the new material by noon tomorrow then, Mr. Freeman?'

'I should think so.'

'We are obliged to you, Mr. Freeman.'

A little wartime poem was surfacing from my subconscious memory; from that mighty iconoclast, that mysterious and comforting leveller.

Last words don't matter. Not her kind of poem; not her speed at all.

And there are none to flatter. False, I suppose. So much notoriety, a name worn smooth as a Victorian penny; surely that was her truest flattery.

Words will not fill the post
Of Leila, ghost

My transposition. Oh Leila, I prayed, substantial shade, whose elements were earth and fire, who haunted me in life, let me be, now you are dead.

What could three hundred words say of Leila? Or three hundred thousand?

Three might do; three that even Leila could not deny, though she could deny most things. I loved her. Yes, even Leila would have gone along with that.

I loved her on a precise day in Marston Mauditt when we lay together for the seventh time in our lives in the conjunction

13

which is common to gods and dogs, floating in that sensual lake high up in the sierras of lust before you reach the precipitous falls. I remembered catching a filched glimpse of us in the mirror on her dressing table and the shock of seeing her naked thighs so shamelessly wide in welcome and my male flesh, in ordinary life so meek and mild, grown monstrous and glowing as I went gently into her glistening body. I remembered the sly female moves she made, those little circular motions of the honest whore, and how there were small globules of sweat in the hollow of her shoulders and an exquisite flush on her face. I remembered her nails greedy in my back and how she cried out my name.

It turned out that the report of her death, like all the others and like Mark Twain's before, was exaggerated.

5   I went up to my hotel room and got out my old brief-
     case. In it I always kept some old maps and guide
     books. Together they make up a tattered testament
to an unquiet life; collectively a private talisman; maps of
Washington, Tel-Aviv, Cairo, and Moscow; obsolescent maps
of unfinished motorways and auto-routes; superannuated
Michelins, guides to Roman villas and holy places. I took out
the map of Marston Mauditt in Hampshire, England.

It's not so much a map as a plan. The scale is six inches to
3000 feet, with an inset showing our old farm in the scale of one
to two thousand five hundred. The agents had coloured the
acres for the 1933 sale with various pleasing water-colours —
apple greens, pinks, soft blues, and ochres. It was a huge estate
before they parcelled it up; as it was, the auction went on for a
week and realised a million pounds in the days when a pound
was still worth five dollars.

Our bit in the inset is much smaller — hardly 300 acres. It
was this portion which Lord Voyce settled on his daughter
Vanessa when she married Charles Taverstock in 1906. It was
not much of a settlement but then he was not much of a catch,
and the upper class bring their invisible, inherited computers
into action when allocating their property.

I loathed the Taverstocks then. I still do, so it's not much use
looking to me for an objective assessment of them. They
employed my grandfather, William Freeman, as their bailiff
throughout his working life, and neither he nor I ever saw any
reason to change our minds about them. True, my grandfather
never talked about it, but then he didn't have to do so; the
facts spoke for themselves. From soon after sunrise till often
after sunset, six days a week, all days except holy days, he toiled
the better part of forty years for them, and I don't believe in all
that time he had any proper thanks for it. Colonel Taverstock

15

was one of those brick-faced, block-headed Englishmen who had been disqualified from any kind of competitive life by his upbringing. Even the rank was somewhat bogus. He had been given it for running an officers' training corps in the First World War. He had no taste, no money, no brains, no humour, no imagination; only a discreet collection of erotica which he had inherited from his wife's father. Lady Vanessa was handsome, vain, and snobbish; she did of course have money or it is unlikely there would have been any marriage. They got on well. At any rate they were never seen to quarrel in public. Their only son, Lionel, died in action on the Somme. Perhaps if he had lived it would have been different.

I doubt if they ever saw *The Admirable Crichton*, which was first produced four years before their marriage. Even if they had, I doubt if it would have dawned on them that my grandfather was far more intelligent and unquantifiably more able than Taverstock. William Freeman was a tall, easily-paced man with blond hair and blue, Norseman's eyes; evidently some kind of Scandinavian throwback. He was an intellectual manqué who introduced me to Thomas Hardy and devoured Beethoven symphonies on his wireless. He was born the year that *Far From The Madding Crowd* was published, yet he might well have read *Jude the Obscure* as a young man when it first came out twenty-two years later. All I know for sure is that he knew Hardy backwards. He was the last contented man I met, and earned no more in a week than I spend on lunch.

Since it turned on Taverstock's whim whether they worked or starved, the Freemans treated him with distant deference. There was precious little understanding in the relationship, scant respect, and no affection whatsoever.

Yet it was a good piece of earth, even under Taverstock. Its soil was the colour of chocolate, its orchards murmurous and heavy with fruit, and at harvest time there was home-brewed cider to replace the sweat that ran down our backs and home-made rabbit pie for our huge hungers. We shot the little palpitating creatures as the threshing machine turned in tighter and tighter circles towards the middle of the field; finally they would make a bolt for it, the shotguns would finish them off, and they would lie still beside the last green excrement of their panic-stricken stomachs. I hardly remember the Colonel and the strange whooping cry with which he would call my grandfather, for all the world as if he were summoning some wild creature of the veld, but I remember going to his funeral when I was ten, an obscure festival of glass and brass, and then Lady Vanessa's widowhood, her chaise-longue beneath the rhododendrons, her china tea and Oliver biscuits, her needlework and her novels from the twopenny library. Whenever I think of her — which is not very often — a phrase from MacNeice chimes through my head: *The inter-ripple and resonance of years of dinner gongs*.

The thirties at Marston Mauditt seemed to roll away in slow motion, and if the war and Adolf Hitler and the Nuremberg decrees meant anything to her she never mentioned it.

> *The lady of the house poises*
> *the silver tongs*
> *And picks a lump of sugar, 'ne plus ultra' she says*
> *I cannot do otherwise, even to prolong my days.*

And one day in the summer of 1943, as the Allies were punching their way into Sicily and Mussolini fell, her days ran out too.

That autumn the house stood desolate. It was an anxious time for my grandfather. He had been left £100 a year for life under her will, but could have no say in his own future. Everything turned on the new owner of Marston Mauditt. Occasionally a prospective purchaser would drive down on black-market petrol, look over the place, and drive away again. In September when I went back to school the house had still not been sold. One day in December, however, my grandfather wrote to me in his immaculate copperplate:

Marston Mauditt has a new owner. He will be quite a change from the last. We have had a talk and I am to continue as bailiff. He is Professor Sir Jakub Haven, the Nobel Prize-winner. His wife Kitty is Ekaterina Tsevetayeva, the famous musician. They will be living at Marston Mauditt with their daughter. Her name is Leila.

17

6 My parents were away in India, where my father, an early meritocrat, was an accountant, and there was no question of seeing them till the end of the war. They had found me a small, dim school in deepest Dorset where I was a boarder. Fortunately my school life forms no part in this story, and the school obtruded only in the negative sense that it kept me away from home two-thirds of the year.

Turning out the cellar last week, we came across the black leather trunk which I used in those days to take my things to and from school. It still has the old G.W.R. labels on it: Kings Scrunton to Marston Mauditt, Marston Mauditt to Kings Scrunton, Marston Mauditt to Oxford via Reading, Oxford back again. It was second-hand when we bought it from Lady Vanessa. Yes, we bought it, and the old bitch charged us a pound for it. It's too heavy for air travel, and today it's full of rubbish. Yet the sight of it brought back with a thump the taste of that journey home and the strange pre-cognition of something unencompassed and disturbing at the end of it. I even remember — or have convinced myself that I remember — the rime on the meadows and the rippling tinsel of the little rivers along which we clattered. The journey is detached, clarified, ratified, in my memory by some rogue trick of the mind. People talk much now of urban sprawl, but even today that fifty mile parallelogram of land which then bounded my total experience unfolds when viewed from the air like one mighty million-acre estate; it's never been so well cared for. I am no sentimentalist about country matters and every year I need the comforts and illusions of the city every so often to off-set the unspecified cruelty in the countryside which now repels me; yet then it seemed innocent enough, no more than a bland backdrop tinted in caramel and apple-green against which to unfold the minor comedy of my youth.

I was nearly eighteen, a white, Anglo-Saxon, protestant, public-school, cock-virgin, pure peasant by descent, middle-class by education, conventionally radical and, as I now see it, unrelentingly boring. Though, to be fair to myself, it would have been difficult to be much else with that background, at least without the springheels of some giant talent, and I had precious little of that. Even the radicalism was no more than a galli-maufry of received ideas from *Picture Post* and *Penguin New Writing*. Has any English public-school radical ever truly broken out of his class? If Orwell couldn't really earn the absolution of a grateful working class, what hope would there be for poor young Ben, who had hardly left it?

My grandfather met me at the station with the Austin, for which we had a small agricultural ration of petrol. It was his own car; he serviced and repaired it himself and it ran like a sewing machine. Whenever I hear the archaic word gentleman I think of him. Since those days I've met three dukes: the first was a definitive moron, the second an amiable cypher, and the third a titanic shit. None of the three could approach my grand-father in natural aristocratic grace.

My grandmother Rosanna Freeman, too, to my mind, always behaved much more like a duchess than any duchess I've ever met. The pair of them, to use another archaic word, had about them some quality of courtliness which they could not transmit to my father; as he moved up an economic class he seemed, in some odd sense, to drop one socially.

I should not like to convey the notion that my grandfather was a paragon. His horizon, despite the books, was by defini-tion limited. He could be intolerant and inflexible, and he was an appalling xenophobe. No, phobia is too strong; but he had the customary Englishman's distrust of and alarm at abroad. He had been no further than Flanders in the First World War where his work as a driver had mercifully kept him away from the front. He thought the French untrustworthy and the Germans uncouth. When the Taverstocks acquired an Italian cook he found it immensely comic and immediately dubbed him Old Macaroni — deeply offending my priggish and jejune internationalist ideals.

'Hello, boy, welcome home.' That bucolic speech, full of long vowels and even longer silences, rich in dipthongs if short on aspirates, is no accent to me, but standard English as it was to Shakespeare. How outlandish and effeminate would BBC twitter have sounded to him too!

'Hello, Grandfather. Good to see you.' The trunk was swung in, and we were on our way.

'The new man has arrived. Different kettle of fish altogether.'

'What's he like?'

'Clever sort of fellow. Well, of course he's clever, Nobel Prize and all. But he looks clever too.'

'What about her?'

'Don't make her out yet. Different from the other one.'

'That's no bad thing.'

'No. Free and easy, you might say. Friendly. No side.'

'Good. What about the girl?'

'Leila? Funny sort of name. Russian or Persian or some such outlandish thing. Nice little girl. Pert, I'd say. Knows a thing or two.'

Grandmother confirmed his judgment: 'They'll be different all right. They're not landed folk. Look as if they've never seen a tree or a cow before. They're friendly and pleasant, but very strange folk for us to get along with.'

'How about the girl, Grandma?'

She looked at me steadily with those violet eyes for which no compromise was possible. 'We shall see about the girl.'

I climbed upstairs to unpack. It was a simple cottage, about a hundred years old, basically two rooms up and two down, but with an outhouse attached which provided a spare bedroom, one of those cool country larders with a flagstone floor, and a workshed. There was no bathroom then, and there was an earth lavatory at the end of the garden. I had the front bedroom, which looked down onto the sundial and kitchen garden. It contained a wardrobe, a chair, a Victorian flower painting, and an immense feather bed. There was a jug and wash-basin, too, and a chamber pot, and the room always smelled faintly of lavender. There was a calendar on the wall which showed a picture of a cottage much like ours. Under it was a verse:

> *God hath not promised*
> *Skies ever blue*
> *Flower strewn pathways*
> *Ever for you*

But he hath promised
Help from above
Unfailing sympathy
Undying love

I've slept in many grander rooms since then, but nothing so voluptuously warm, so comfortingly womb-like as that magnificent bed on a midwinter's night. In a centrally heated world you have no experience of the old teeth-chattering chills, but then again, you have no true pleasure in the warmth either; not that delight in hiding from the elemental cold which the human animal shares with the whole brute creation. It was the sort of bed in which it would have been a mortal sin not to make love.

I had indeed made love there to a broad spectrum of the world's most intoxicating women: Ingrid Bergman, Hedy Lamarr, Lana Turner, my housemaster's wife, the amply-bosomed girl in the school bookshop — it was a massive list of conquests, and increased nightly as my imagination rioted in that indescribably libidinous cocoon.

I washed in the caressingly soft rainwater which they collected in a stout butt by the back door — another incalculable luxury lost to urban man — and came down to lardy cake and china tea before a log fire which hissed with sap and filled the little room with its smoky fragrance. My grandfather had gone back to the cares of the farm; my grandmother was busy in her kitchen; I reached a languid hand to the bookshelf for the delight of Thomas Hardy's company. There was a tap at the front door, and when I went to open it, a girl was standing there with a basket. 'Hello,' she said. 'I'm Leila.'

7 She was my age; not very tall but curiously sturdy. Her hair, glinting in the December sun, was the colour of Chablis and cut short. She had a broad face with high cheekbones, pale skin and green eyes. She wore a sweater and a tweed skirt and flat shoes; her hands were square and well kept, without varnish; indeed she wore little make-up, then or at any time. Her voice though; each sentence sounded a little as if her heart was breaking, even when she was just asking you to pass the salt. She had been brought up by a Finnish nurse, I discovered later, and had fortunately never quite thrown off the Scandinavian vowels, so that English as spoken by her had a haunting undertow that set the senses sighing, however plain the subject matter.

'Hello. I'm Ben Freeman. Do come in.'

'How do you do, Ben. Thanks. My mother's been sent some caviare for Christmas, and she thought you might like some.'

It was going to be a new style all right.

'That's very kind of you.'

'It came from friends in America. God knows where they get it from.'

'I don't believe I've ever tasted it.'

'You'll like it. I could eat it by the pound.'

'How do you eat it?'

'Lots of ways. I like it on crushed ice, with thin pieces of dry toast and lemon wedges and hard-boiled egg crushed through a sieve.'

'I'm afraid we don't have a refrigerator here.'

'No. How thoughtless of me. Come up to the house and I'll show you how it's done.'

I called out to my grandmother, 'Leila's brought us some caviare.' She appeared, wiping her hands, her expression comically bemused.

22

'That's very kind of you, I'm sure, Miss.'

'And now, if you'll allow me, Mrs. Freeman, I'll take him up to our kitchen and show him how to serve it to you.'

'Very well then. Now behave yourself, Ben.'

We strolled up the pathway towards the big house. I carried the jar of caviare as if it were a small time-bomb. Leila said: 'That was a bloody silly idea.'

'The caviare? Let them eat cake, you mean?'

'Yes, that sort of thing. My mother, of course, regards it much like bread. Most Russians do.'

'I think it was very nice of your mother.'

'You haven't met her yet?'

'No. Nor your father.'

'They're both very harmless.'

We went into the kitchen of the big house. It was a generous, warm room, with a long open-range stove and wide working areas, festooned with wholesome copper pots and pans. Here I had passed many warm and languorous hours in my childhood watching my grandmother cook for the Taverstocks, and, when she was not there, listening to Oliver Debenham, the chauffeur, relate his seamy adventures with previous employers who had used the newfound mobility of the motor car as a launching pad for seduction. Oliver was a burly and cynical fellow of thirty-three or four who was the nearest I had been to a man of the world. He was engaged to Millicent Brownjohn, the maid, a healthy, plump young girl whom he showed no great enthusiasm to make into an honest woman. It was Leila who first dubbed them Debenham and Freebody — a fairly obvious joke, but not one that had occurred to me or, of course, to my grandparents, though I am bound to say they both quite enjoyed it. The Havens had acquired Debenham and Freebody with the house, and indeed Debenham was already seated at the table, drinking his ninth or tenth cup of tea of the day — another free commodity to which he had become entitled by long usage. He rose when we arrived, not being totally sure yet of his new relationship with his employers.

'Hello, Oliver,' said Leila, 'Have some caviare.'

Oliver's expression was a good mirror image of my grandmother's.

'Caviare, Miss? Don't believe I ever tried it. Though come to think of it, a gent I used to drive for in London before the war was very partial to it. Used to give it to his young ladies with a bottle of Bollinger to wash it down. Worked a treat he used to say.'

'Well, we shall see what effect it has on your Milly. Find me a couple of lemons, there's a dear girl.'

Milly obliged, toast was made, and we settled ourselves round the table to try the forbidden fruit of the sturgeon. 'No, wait,' Leila jumped up. 'We must do the thing properly.' She disappeared into the dining room. Oliver gave me and Millicent what used to be called an old-fashioned look.

'We're in for some fun and games,' he adjudicated.

Leila returned with a bottle of vodka and some small glasses.

It was four o'clock in the afternoon.

'Now,' said Leila, 'we are complete.'

Oliver raised his glass. 'Your good health, Miss.'

'Yours, Oliver.'

It was at this moment that I first had the curious sensation of sitting in the middle of the stage during a Chekhov play; and the image, once fixed, never left me while the Havens lived at Marston Mauditt. For them, employers and servants were not really separate classes; they were all members of a large amorphous family in which each personality had a vital part to play. They genuinely preferred the kitchen to any other part of the house, though they used the dining room when they had important visitors. They were totally unselfconscious and did not seem aware of the English class system. They treated us, in short, like human beings, with some curious consequences.

'To be truthful, I don't honestly know why it's so cracked up, Miss,' said Oliver after his third mouthful.

'It's an acquired taste,' said Leila. 'You'll get to the stage when you can't do without it.'

'Lord, it's gone to my head,' said Milly. 'I feel quite tipsy and I've still got the vegetables to do for dinner.'

'Here, I'll help you,' said Leila.

'Heavens no, Miss. What will Lady Kitty say?'

'I know what she'll say if there are no vegetables.'

They worked side by side.

When I got back to the cottage much later, bearing with me a plate of the caviare freshly iced and seasoned, I felt distinctly lightheaded. My grandparents did not care for the dish.

'Funny tasting stuff,' said my grandmother, 'like a lot of little seeds.'

'They are seeds,' I told her, 'or at any rate, eggs. You should really have it with vodka.'

'Take a bit of getting used to,' said my grandfather, but whether he meant the caviare or the Havens, I didn't know. Very probably both.

8 It's pretty well accepted that the war, which killed, maimed, and bereaved so many millions, brought unquantifiable benefits to millions more. People made money, got promoted, travelled, found themselves faced with unimagined changes and opportunities. I was among the lucky millions: just too young to be killed off, just old enough to find myself. The war brought Mme. Tassigli to teach French to the sixth form at my school while her husband was working with de Gaulle; and this magnificent woman made my head sing with French poetry so that it echoes to this day. She filled my imagination with the picture of a country I had never visited, but which was ruled by clarity, logic, taste and wit. Later I was to find that this was merely one view of France and by no means a three-dimensional one. Never mind, it served then, and so magical was the pull of that ugly, lovely woman that I spoke French well enough when I left school to gain my only distinction in the oral part of my final examination and it was that which led to Interpreter's School and so to my eventual career.

If it had not been for the war I should not have been living at Marston Mauditt and nor would Leila: they bought the place for peace from the bombing. And so on. Yet, more than this; in the total bracket of one's life, the war was vitally important because it heightened the quality of experience. Every new impression was keener, sharper, cleaner; the threat of death concentrated the mind wonderfully. Most of the war I didn't think we'd win and it was Mme Tassigli who gave me heart when we discussed it one day. 'My dear boy' — I can still hear her mocking me, 'even if they managed to land, you don't seriously think we'd let them get this far?' She made the threat seem so ridiculous, that I was ashamed and put the fear from my mind.

I know from an old diary that it was two days later that I first heard Leila play the piano. I'd been working at a French prose, one of the half-dozen Mme. Tassigli had given me to translate over the holiday, and tiring of the complicated and rather dry text she'd given me, I wandered up the pathway towards the big house. Since our first meeting, I'd not seen Leila, though to be truthful I'd several times taken a turn round the grounds in the hope that I might bump into her.

To get to the house you could either go the short way or by a winding path that took you through the copse and along the side of Marston lake. I went the long way that night, with moonlight spilling on me through the bare branches. It was soft underfoot, and still above; a stillness whose effect was multiplied many times because it was snatched from the midst of war; often at Marston Mauditt we heard the thunder of the guns from the south coast and the farm was lit by the flash of distant bombs. This night, though, there was nothing of war in the midwinter sky. I came at last into the clearing where the lawn began; gradually it broadened out to accommodate the southern wing of the house, with its 1840-ish French windows that in days of peace cast their ochre light on the gambollings of the Taverstocks at play. Tonight, the curtains were drawn, but there was a chink through which I could peep at the scene inside.

Leila was alone at the piano, and she was playing something which has since become part of the equity of my mind; then, though, it was new, a great series of rippling and clustered chords, brilliant, fierce, and glorious to hear. They went on for an incalculable time; then she paused, looked up but did not see me, and began the second movement. This was very slow and lyrical, totally simple and pure. As she played it, I fell in love, not only with Leila, who did not, as it later transpired, believe in my kind of love, but also with the world as a place where such music was possible; a world in fact only underwritten and guaranteed, made whole by it. It became, if you like, my tune.

The music stopped and I turned to go, tripped over one of my grandfather's low wire fences and fell, with an almighty crash, flat on my face. Leila, disturbed, came to the curtains, drew them back and undid the French windows.

'Shit!'

27

'Ben! My dear boy, what are you doing there?'

'I'm sorry, Leila, I couldn't help listening to you, and I fell over this wire fence.'

She laughed. 'Poor Ben! Here let me help you.' She took my handkerchief from me and wiped my muddy face with it, her eyes still laughing.

'I'm afraid it wasn't worth it, was it?'

'I thought it was.'

'I like to play to myself sometimes. I meant to be a pianist but my parents thought I'd never be good enough.'

'You sounded pretty good to me but I didn't recognise it.'

'It's the Beethoven C Minor Sonata, Number 8. But not concert standard. That's the trouble with my family, you have to excel or drop out. That's the rule. God, what a beautiful night!' She had taken in the benediction of the contraband moonlight.

'I was just having a break from translating.'

'Take me for a walk, Ben.'

'Of course.'

She got a coat and we set off, and as we walked she put her arm through mine.

'This clearing in the wood was made by my grandfather to sow the lawn. Once, the trees ran right up to the house.'

'I had the idea that it had been here for at least two hundred years.'

'Twenty. But he made it well, didn't he?' She stopped and turned towards me. Then she said:

'The sight of the clearing brings tears to her eyes,
She remembers the birches that flourished there.'

I said, 'How did you know?'

She hesitated, 'About the birches?'

'Yes. The place was thick with birches.'

'I didn't know. That's a poem by a Russian writer called Nekrasov.'

'I'm afraid I don't know any Russian poetry.'

Another pause. Then she said, ' "Who in Russia lives a care-free life?" That's Nekrasov, too.'

'I wish I knew more Russian writers. I love Chekhov.'

'You would have to be a desperate philistine not to.'

'I'm haunted by everything he writes. Such simplicity. "I'm in mourning for my life." And the last line too — "Konstantin

Gavrilovich has shot himself." What courage, to end a play like that!'

'You know it was booed off the stage when it was first performed at Petersburg?'

'No, I didn't.'

'He swore he'd never write another play. And then Stanislavsky took it over, and produced it at the Moscow Art Centre, and it was a smash hit.'

'Once they understood it.'

'Yes. But the curious thing is that Stanislavsky didn't understand it. He produced it as a tragedy.'

'Well, isn't it a tragedy?'

'Of course not. He called it a comedy in four acts. You can't take that last line seriously, can you?'

'I don't know how to take it.'

'Exactly. It's outside language.'

'I felt, in the kitchen the other day, as if we were in a play by Chekhov. It was because you were there.'

Leila threw back her head and laughed.

'My dear Ben! What flattery!'

'Still, I did.'

'So you think this house is a set for a play by Chekhov?'

'With you in it, yes.'

'I know what you mean. But if you think that, you must come one day to our house in Finland if — '

I waited.

'If it still exists. It may well not. But if not, we shall build it again. The winter war, you know, was very cruel to the Finnish people.'

'I didn't know you were Finnish.'

'A quarter. My mother's mother was Finnish, her father Russian. We always went to Finland before the war. We had a house not too far from the Russian border, by the sea. In winter it was frozen, and covered with snow like an endless white plain. We were on the edge of a forest, and we used to go into it every day to pick wild mushrooms and a special red cranberry. There was a big granary outside, where all the people used to come for parties in the summer, and we hung lanterns in the trees.'

'And is it true that you have this boiling hot bath and are beaten with twigs and then jump into the snow?'

'Absolutely. But my dear Ben, it's not as frightful as you think. First, the sauna is dry heat, and as such you can stand far more than when the air is moist. Half an hour in the sauna smoothes out your soul. And, then, those twigs — they're deliciously soft, you know. Almost caressing.'

'How about the snow then?'

'It's a delight. You see, you're so hot by that time that you're insulated from the cold. Of course if you stayed outside stark naked for half an hour, you'd be a block of ice. But you don't.'

'And is it true that men and women take saunas together?'

'Sure. It's a totally non-sexual ceremony. There's only one quite unforgivable sin in a sauna, and that is to fart.'

'I see.'

We had completed our walk along the park, and had arrived back at the lawn in front of the house.

'The sight of the clearing brings tears to her eyes,' I said involuntarily and Leila took up the next line:

'She remembers the birches that flourished there. Good night, Ben.'

She kissed me on the mouth and was gone. It was a light kiss, yet not the kind you write off. It lingered as I strolled reflectively back to my grandparents' cottage; it lingers to this day.

9 The fact is, I had a girl at Marston Mauditt already. Her name was Sue Carter, and her father was the local builder Joseph Carter, a right villain but an amusing one. She and I had grown up together. She was a few months older than I, already eighteen, and had just begun studying to be a secretary. She was dark, with her father's black hair and Spanish eyes, a strapping girl who never quite knew how to finish a sentence. I liked her then and I like her now; though she lives three thousand miles away we still write to each other and I'm the godfather of one of her children. Sue was destined to be one of the world's losers, and you felt you had to do what you could to protect her even when she was at her most exasperating. She loved dogs and horses, Byron and Benny Goodman, and for a while I think, me. Her mother, Cynthia, was thought to have come down in the world somewhat through marrying Joe Carter. Joe drove a Riley even in wartime, and was a bosom friend of the local police chief, Inspector Tripp. He drank pink gins and was an excellent shot. I used to admire his hand-made cream silk shirts and custom-built tweed suits. He was not too worried about the niceties of the law, never went without butter, eggs, and steaks at the height of rationing, and I daresay might well have ended up in a prison on black market offences if he hadn't been such a pal of Inspector Tripp. He had been the contractor who built R.A.F. Herriott Wood, our nearest bomber station, which must have made his fortune, but Cynthia had money too. She always reminded me of a Michael Arlen heroine, and indeed she had once lived in Shepherd Market. They didn't entertain much, but used to go away to their caravan at the weekend leaving the house in charge of their housekeeper, Mrs Rollister, whose husband was in prison. It was an archetypal 1930s house, the kind you see in those conscientious dramatisations of Huxley novels; it was apple green

31

and tasselled and always seemed to me to be adorned with silver statuettes of naked nymphs, though surely my memory is having me on. There were plenty of novels by Dornford Yates, if you liked that sort of thing, and records of Weber, Ravel, and Gershwin. The Carters were unfailingly kind to me, and why two such basically generous human beings should be so mistrusted I didn't then understand, though I supposed there was something slightly too fast and *louche* about them for the villagers to follow.

Sue used to send letters to me at school which I looked forward to immensely, with their news of shows like *Oklahoma!* and singers like Jean Sablon, and I remember sending her some nylons for her eighteenth birthday which were a sensational success. She had one dress I used to love, a peasant smock the colour of buttercups, a style which curiously enough is back in fashion again thirty years later as I write this. It had the mysterious effect of making her seem both fragile and earthy. When Mrs Rollister had gone to bed we used to lie on the couch close together in front of the log fire and exchange long cinematic kisses, her magnificent bosom strained against the smock, and I with a mighty hard on. Yet comical as it must now seem, the affair had never got any further than that.

I had a rival, though. Toby Henderson had lived at the White House in Marston Mauditt ever since I could remember. His father was the local brewer, and their property ran down to the boundary of my grandparents' kitchen garden. A tall hedge marked the division, but a boy could crawl under it easily enough. Toby and I had been friends of a sort since infancy; but he was a year older than I and moved in a much more sophisticated world. The word *cad* has now effectively passed out of the English language; Toby was a quintessential cad and hence peculiarly fascinating to a naïve youth like myself.

I saw *cad* defined recently as a gentleman who has given up his code; the definition fitted Toby precisely. The word went full cycle in its hundred years of life; first used at Oxford to describe townsmen or literal outsiders, it imperceptibly came to mean someone who had been taught all the rules but had decided to break them. Nobody believes much in rules any more; we are all cads now. In that curious twilight world of the 1940s, though, the old values sporadically flickered on, though the truth is that the immense winds of change which were to extinguish them for ever were already at play, only we didn't know it.

A cad looked like a gentleman, dressed like a gentleman, spoke like a gentleman, but did not, in the end, behave like a gentleman. He was the officer who was cashiered, the clergyman who was defrocked, the stockbroker who was hammered, the lawyer who was disbarred, the doctor who was struck off the register — note how the English have a multiplicity of terms to denote the expulsion of the maverick from the club. When John Profumo felt obliged to resign from his club he was going through the classic ritual of the dishonoured gentleman; but the year was 1963 and it was far too late for that kind of gesture: unnecessary, irrelevant, meaningless, and comically sad. He's joined again now and no one noticed or cared.

Toby was one of the last great cads. He was a big lad, just over six feet and at eighteen already running to fat. He had a smooth pink face, blond hair plastered straight back, slightly protruding ears, and well-manicured little hands. He drank pink gins and kept Balkan Sobranie in a silver cigarette case. After leaving his preparatory school he had gone to Osborne and Dartmouth, and was due home on leave this Christmas before being posted to his first ship. I quite looked forward to seeing him, for he was always good company, though you had to take him in fairly small doses, and keep him off the vast subterranean folk-lore of the Royal Navy, otherwise you were done for.

Toby may have been a homosexual, despite his subsequent career. He certainly made one or two overt passes at me in his teens, but that may have been part of the normal English boarding school syndrome. I remained irrevocably and perhaps almost priggishly heterosexual, though now I look back from this vantage-point thirty years later, I recognise that one or two balloons of emotional experiences that I thought were categories of ordinary male friendship may have had an ambiguous content.

Sue's attitude to Toby seemed to fluctuate in a bewildering and, to me, incomprehensible manner. Most of the time she thought he was appalling; but occasionally he'd come home in his midshipman's uniform and take her off to a night club in London. On these sorties she always seemed flattered by his interest and I, a mere schoolboy, and a broke one at that, could only watch full of impotent and baleful rage. At such moments I hated Toby. However, he was not due home till the next day and so I hurried round to Sue's house to pay my attention while I could.

Sue and Cynthia were in the kitchen making steak and chips with some black market eggs for Joe's supper.

'Hello, Ben,' said Cynthia. 'You're looking all pale and interesting.'

'Shut up, he's mine,' said Sue. She gave me a big friendly kiss.

'He reminds me of a boyfriend I once had in the navy,' said Cynthia. 'Teddy. He was lovely. All blond and scrumptious. But he went down with the *Ark Royal*.'

'And that only left Pa.'

'Don't be beastly. Pa's all right. How's school Ben?'

'Not bad, thank you, Mrs. Carter.'

'And your grandparents?'

'They're fine too.'

'What are the new people like at the big house?'

'They seem nice. He's a scientist. The mother's Russian.'

'There's a girl too,' said Sue.

'Yes. Leila.'

'Oh, so you've met her?' Sue asked quickly.

'Yes.'

'What's she like?' They both said it.

'Quite small and sturdy. Green eyes. Like a Russian peasant.'

'How do you know what a Russian peasant's like?' asked Sue suspiciously.

'Because I've seen them in all those Russian war films.'

'But is she nice?' asked Cynthia.

'Well she's certainly friendly. She gave me some caviare.'

'Well you won't get any caviare here,' said Sue. 'You can finish up the chips, though, if you like.' Sue handed over the plate.

'Thanks. I prefer these to caviare.'

'Liar.' That was Sue of course.

'She gave me some vodka too.'

'Cor luvaduck,' said Sue coarsely. She rummaged around in the refrigerator. 'Here you are, lover-boy, wrap yourself round a bottle of Dad's brown ale.'

'Thanks.' I had only just discovered beer.

34

'And don't tell us you prefer it to vodka because we won't believe you.'

'All right. Cheers.'

'What's her figure like?' Sue pursued me.

'I just told you — like a Russian peasant.'

'Not that, dope. What sort of bosom has she got?'

'I didn't really notice.'

'Un-noticeable bosom,' said Cynthia. 'Can't be too lethal.'

'He probably hasn't even noticed mine,' said Sue moodily.

'Of course I have.'

'Ben Freeman,' said Sue, 'you are a notorious drip. Where are we going tonight?'

'I thought we might see *Orchestra Wives* at the Palace.'

'Super.'

And so we passed the evening in the company of Miller's mellifluous trombones and his row of saxes with the clarinet swinging sweetly up above. When we got to the gate of Sue's house we kissed and somewhat unexpectedly she put her tongue in my mouth for the first time.

'Bet she doesn't do that,' said Sue.

Toby appeared next morning. He banged once on the back door of our cottage, then marched in, as he usually did. 'What-ho, Ben, old fruit!' he greeted me.

'Hello, Toby. Gosh you look very crisp this morning.'

'Like it? Got it from Gieves, the naval tailors.' He had acquired a tweed hacking jacket in a large houndstooth check, which he wore with a pair of cavalry twill trousers and brown suede boots. 'All right for point-to-points and that sort of caper. How are things in this pisshole of a place?'

'Much the same. The new people have arrived at the big house.'

'So I hear.' Toby's usually bland and epicene features darkened. 'I've been talking to Dad about them. Pretty rum crew. Lot of reds I gather.'

'Nothing unusual in that. Most scientists are socialists.'

'Not socialists, twat. Reds. Communists. Bolshies. The full gubbins.'

'Oh. I didn't know that.'

'Wife's a Russian. God knows what they're up to.'

'Aren't we on the same side?'

'Don't be so naïve, Ben, lad. Can't trust them further than you can throw them.'

'But I thought Professor Haven was a boffin — helping the war effort and all that.'

'Helping the Russkies no doubt. Probably sold all our secrets to them already.'

'I find that hard to believe.'

'You find anything hard to believe, Ben my boy. But I could tell you a thing or two if my lips weren't sealed by the Official Secrets Act. Incidentally, we've just learned a new wardroom toast. It goes like this: "Mr. Vice, I looks towards you — " '

'The girl seems rather nice.'

'Leila? Fast little bitch, I gather. Mother heard she was sacked from Cambridge, and God knows you've got to be pretty seedy to be thrown out of a place like that.'

'I hadn't heard that.'

'The trouble with you, young master Ben, is that you haven't heard anything. Done anything about your call-up yet?'

'No. I'm going along to the Labour Exchange this holiday.'

'That's it. No slacking now. It'll make a man of you. Put some gravel in your guts.'

'I thought I might have a shot at an interpreter's course.'

'Pretty soft option, Ben. Don't you fancy a spot of real fighting?'

'Not much. Anyway, it'll all be over before I can do much about it. Thank God.'

'The Hun's days are numbered. But we can still have a crack at the Jap. That'll take time, Ben. That'll be the one to separate the men from the boys.'

'All very well for you in your bloody battleship.'

'Haven't you heard of kamikaze pilots? They go on a special diet of wine, women and song, then off they go loaded to the nines with bombs and only enough fuel for a one-way journey. They come in at you out of the sun so — yaaargh!' His little white hand swooped down menacingly from above his shoulder. 'And kerboom! You've got plane, bombs, and pilot plastered all over your deck. Nasty. Fanatical little buggers. All for the glory of Nippon and the Emperor. Take a year or two to winkle the little yellow bastards out.'

'Banzai!' said a cool female voice just outside the window. Toby leaped to his feet like a startled otter.

'Sorry,' said Leila. 'I couldn't help overhearing.' She leaned

36

over the sill, and yet again I saw and remembered the winter sunlight glinting in her hair.

'Leila,' I said, 'this is Toby, a friend of mine. He lives next door in the White House.'

'How do you do, Toby,' said Leila. Toby had gone salmon pink, but whether from embarrassment or excitement I could not tell.

'How d'ye do. Delighted I'm sure,' he got out. He was not certain how much she had overheard.

'Toby's in the navy,' I explained. 'He's in a battleship.'

'I'm not even sure if I'm going to a battleship,' said Toby suddenly.

'I've always seen you as the quintessential battleship man,' I said truthfully.

'I could go to Light Coastal Forces. That's what we call the private navy. Motor torpedo boats. Seventy feet. Two officers and a crew of eight to fourteen. Then there's a rather bigger boat. The D-type; 120 feet, three officers and a crew of thirty-two. You live on board; the captain's cabin is the size of your average loo. Of course in bigger ships all officers expect a separate cabin.'

'You're regular navy?' Leila hazarded. It was a shrewd guess.

'Lord yes. Straight stripe. None of your wavy navy lark for me, thanks very much. Of course we tend to stick together a bit. Have to, in a way.'

'Tell us about your social customs, Toby,' I said. To invite this subject was the supreme gesture as far as I was concerned. Once out of that trap, he was away like a thoroughbred greyhound.

'Well, we still have guest nights. Wear black tie with number one uniform. The President is the most senior officer present. Then there's a chap at the other end called Mr. Vice. He's the most junior officer present, poor sod. Almost certainly myself for a year or two. When you get to the loyal toast it's not the President who takes it. Absolutely bally not. He taps on the table and says: "Mr. Vice — the King". Then Mr. Vice — that's me, no doubt, poor sod — says in a quavering voice: "Gentlemen the King". Then after dinner, providing there are no ladies present' — with a sickly inclination towards Leila — 'we play a few silly games like stripping the willow. Then there's another game where you buy a chap a bottle of something and you get him to drink it while everyone sings "drink chug-a-lug, chug-a-lug, chug-a-lug . . ." You have to understand the flags of course. There's one called pennant nine. It's green, white and green, and basically it means we're having a party, everyone's welcome. Very popular pennant, I can tell you.'

Throughout his monologue Toby had been self-consciously twisting a brown paper parcel that he was carrying. He now shyly undid it, and produced a naval officer's cap.

'Got this today. Course, it's much too new. What us young officers do is to jump on them a few times to make them feel lived-in.' So saying he threw the hat on the floor and proceeded to trample it energetically with his feet. A faint smell of mothballs permeated the room. Soon the hat looked appropriately battered.

'You're supposed to wear it absolutely straight,' Toby told us, putting it on precisely plumb. 'But us young officers like to wear it at a slight angle so — ' he demonstrated. 'We call it the Beatty tilt, after Admiral Beatty who always wore his hat like that.'

'What a pretty way you've found to kill,' said Leila.

10 June 1944 was a pretty good time for everyone in Europe unless, of course, you happened to be German. It was the month that the Allies landed again in France to stay and, on the 15th, that the V1 and V2 rockets began to fall on England so giving us, mixed irrevocably together among the first blossom, the stir of life and the chance of death. I came home on the 17th, so my diary reminds me, full of Hugo and de Musset and Theophile Gautier and, above all such echoes from a frozen, encapsulated past, the ever-present thought of Leila. She met me at the station in her parents' Humber and kissed me again on the lips. She told me the news as we crunched up the hill to Marston Mauditt: her father was in America, her mother had been thrilled to hear at last from her family in Russia though they had gone through unimaginable privations, my grandparents were saints, the other scientists who were working with her father on some secret project were all bores. She was, she affirmed, so pleased to see me.

It was a time of hope amid the last heart-catching fears. Even down there, in that cradle nursed by silence and time, we sometimes heard the drone of the V-bombs, and then that terrible moment when their motors cut, and then the shake and thunder of their landing. Still, we all seemed to know that it was the last act of the European war that was being played out. The sun beat down on the roof of the Humber as we drove, and was refracted through the hedgerows.

'Ben,' she said again. 'It's so good to see you.'

'You too.' All the majesty of French literature could not help me find any other words.

'As soon as you've said hello to your grandparents you must come to see my flat. It's ready — or as ready as it will ever be.'

There was the obligatory tea and lardy cake in the cottage. I gulped it down and made my excuses.

Leila's flat was in fact the upper half of our old stables. Below, the horses had once been kept; above the grooms, when the Taverstocks had been able to afford them, had once slept. She had taken two of these simple rooms and knocked down the adjoining wall, so making a big attic in which she had built shelves for her books and hung pictures — father, mother, her favourite Finnish nurse and her favourite uncle Bruno — on the slatted wooden walls. She had installed a tiny kitchen there, and brought her gramophone and records. When the trap-door was pulled up and secured, you felt totally safe, secure, enclosed; the raw facts of life shut outside.

She was reading when I arrived and knocked awkwardly on the trap-door.

'Oh, Ben, I thought you would never come. Here, give me your hand.'

She pulled me up into the loft.

'Leila, you've done wonders with it. I remember it up here as a disaster.

'Soap and water and elbow grease. You really like it?'

'I love it. Will you live here?'

'I do. It's my castle. My independence.'

'And your parents don't mind?'

She shook her head. 'It's near enough after all. And I'm nineteen now.'

'I suppose so.'

'Come and sit down, Ben.'

I sat gingerly on her bed. She put her head on my knee. Our hands met.

'See how quiet it is.'

'Yes it is very quiet.'

The Russian farm clock which she had purloined from her parents seemed to tick louder now, filling the room, flooding my mind, counting away the seconds of our lives.

I settled back, still holding her hand. She rested her head on my chest, and placed her fingers lightly on my face.

'His chin, new reaped, showed like a stubble land at harvest home.'

'Sorry, I didn't — '

'Shakespeare or somebody. You're growing up, Ben.'

'Going on nineteen.'

'But in some ways still a child.'

'If you say so.'

She raised her head and kissed me on the lips again. It was as if she were asking me a question and expecting the answer to be yes.

'I still remember the first time you kissed me, Leila.'

'I remember it too.'

She kissed me again, and then to my surprise, a dozen or more times, slowly circumnavigating my eyes, and nose, and ears; then came back to my lips again, though still gently and innocently.

'Does Sue kiss you like this?'

'No.'

'I thought not.'

She gently but deliberately undid the top button of my shirt, and then the next, till it came apart. Then she slowly kissed me in the middle of my chest, and so downwards, while new and urgent messages clamoured alarms along my nerves.

'You're not frightened, Ben?'

'Not at all.' I was petrified, but not prepared to admit it. She left a trail of kisses along my stomach, downy with incipient manhood, but previously untouched. Then she lifted her head and kissed my lips again, and before she did so, I saw that her green eyes were dilated like a cat's, and that a beautiful flush had risen in those high cheekbones. And now her lips were slowly travelling again from my chin to my throat, and from there downwards once more. I held her hand. She glanced up.

'Don't be frightened, Ben.'

'I'm not.' My teeth were chattering, though not altogether with fear. Once she had negotiated the minor hurdle of my leather belt, loosened and freed its metal buckle, she tenderly explored me with her fingers, while the blood sang and pounded in me.

Her hands were warm and careful, establishing their territorial rights by persuasion, not predatory. Then she bent down and began to kiss me again, moving softly down the centre of my young untried male body, and each kiss awaking a new and greater riot in me. When she reached the end of her journey the rage in my nerves seemed to dissolve my mind to the point where I and the erotic play were one continuous experience; there was nothing left to my perception except the silken knowledge of first fellatio. I was drowning in a torrent of new sensa-

41

tions both alien and, yet in some folk-memory, already known, at once comforting and alarming. I closed my eyes as she paid her delicate attentions; I was floating in a sea of pleasure both male and female, hard and yielding, exigent and melting; I was slowly being lifted through one octave of sensation to the next. Then we seemed to have reached some mysterious plateau which unrolled for ever, and I tried to say something, but I had no breath and no words came; and then we had reached the edge of that level place and came plummeting down in a great cascading sequence of sensual arpeggios. I was shaken by a long series of uncontrollable spasms which both ashamed and fulfilled by their overt wildness; and then very slowly the ache dispersed and the storm subsided, and I was back in Leila's room with my eyes full of tears.

For a long time she lay with her head resting on my stomach; then she looked up and smiled at me. 'Hello, Ben,' she said, pushing the hair back from her eyes; and kissed me on the lips once more for luck.

11 Kitty Haven was born Ekaterina Sergeyevna Tsevetayeva at St. Petersburg in 1902. Her father was a doctor and writer on medical subjects; her mother was a gifted singer. Kitty showed signs of precocious musical talent and gave her first public concert when she was sixteen. Her father was active in the liberal revolution of March 1917, a distinction which did not stand him in good stead when the Bolsheviks prevailed, and with her two young brothers and her parents she left Russia for ever in early 1919. She was briefly at the Prague Gymnasium, then at the Berlin Singakademie, and finally settled in Vienna where she met her husband at a friend's house after the opera one evening. They were married in 1924, and lived in Vienna until 1938. They were happy there, but she remained Russian at heart. She had known the young Prokofiev and was a cousin of Ossip Gabrilowitsch, who in turn was the son-in-law, improbably enough, of Mark Twain. Even then, the creative world was a global village. She loved poetry, and the works of Alexander Blok and Andrei Bely were never far from her side. Like all Russians, she had an almost mystical reverence for the earth. Anyone who has ever seen any Russian earth will know how inscrutable this passion is. Though she did not actually kiss the earth on each return from abroad like Nabokov's mother, she cherished it and all its fruits. Her house was always filled with the scent of flowers. The first time I ever heard her perform in public, at a concert in London just after the war, she played the Dvorak Cello Concerto in B minor, Opus 104, with such stunning brilliance that I still hear it in my head and can't go a week without replaying her recording of it.

Her relationship with Leila was just that loving-nagging oscillation one sees between so many only daughters and their mothers. They would gossip endlessly and with limitless pleasure; they would quarrel; they would scream at each other;

43

then kiss and make up. They were in a real sense rivals, for in her early forties Kitty was still capable of scoring a direct hit on any unsuspecting male animal who walked unwarily into the range of her sexual artillery.

I was an early casualty, and at times not certain which of them I loved more. She cared enormously about her body and would spend the first half hour of each day exercising, however late she'd been to bed; then to the amazement of the locals she'd come out of the French windows in a white bathing dress and take a clean header into the lake. After that she would go to her room and play till lunch-time. I often used to steal under her window and listen, for it's not every day you can hear one of the best six cellists in the world. After lunching on yoghourt and fruit she used to call Oliver and go for a brisk drive to Guildford or Winchester where she would rummage through the antique shops or go to auctions. She adored jewellery and wore it with panache; indeed all her parents had brought out of Russia was a handful of necklaces and bracelets and somehow they'd managed to keep them through all the bad times.

Above all, she loved life. 'My God, Ben,' she used to exclaim to me before a party, her pale skin glowing with anticipated delight, 'we shall have fun tonight!' She was brisk and practical in her kindness. Once, she found me in the kitchen after one of her soirées, fragile and bloodshot, my brain peeled open to the elements by too much vodka. She seized a basin and whipped up three raw eggs, then added a lacing of cognac. 'We give this,' she explained, 'to our ballerinas before they make a big jump.' Then she thrust two small white pills into my hand.

'What are these for?' I enquired nervously.

'They are,' she declaimed dramatically, 'for drunkards!'

It worked.

She spoke English with less accent than Leila, having learned it from a string of English governesses in St. Petersburg before she learned Russian. There was a pastel portrait of her, done by Leon Bakst just before they left Russia, which hung in their drawing room; it could have been Leila.

I suppose what I am most grateful to Kitty for is opening my eyes. She enlarged the little lens in my imagination and made it take in the wide screen of the entire possible world. Not only in the literal sense did she make me look at pictures — I first saw the works of Chagall and Kandinsky on her walls — she made

44

me, infinitely more important, look at *her*; the gift of every great courtesan and hostess through the centuries. She taught me manners. I don't mean by this that before I had eaten my peas off my knife — my grandparents had taught me the fundamentals of all that — but she taught me the little grace of the thank you letter. On her birthday — I think it must have been her forty-third though it was hard to believe, so ravishing did she look that day — I sent her a bunch of flowers freshly cut from our cottage garden. From her response, you would have imagined I had sent the crown jewels. She wrote in a very large flowing hand — she was indeed incapable of doing anything on a small scale — and she said:

Dearest Ben,
    Your heavenly flowers have made my day perfect. I have put them on the piano so that I can see them when I play. They are to earth what music is to air — the best evidence we have of a benevolent creator. For surely no imaginable creator could both hate us and give us either flowers or music. Thank you, darling Ben, and believe me when I say that when I played today I played for you alone.
                                    Your loving friend,
                                    Kitty.

Well, I suppose it wouldn't do nowadays. But for a boy of nineteen, and daft with it, that letter had a certain charm. I kept it to this day, otherwise I couldn't have reproduced it so faithfully.
    The fact is that Kitty almost closed — maybe at times she totally closed — that gap which separates the minds of men and women. And when that miraculous fusion does take place — so rarely, but when it does — then love is born. I loved Kitty, as I loved Leila. She is one of the three women I care for most in the world, still, thank heaven, alive, still beautiful, still playing heart-stopping music in Jerusalem, love of my young days, love all the days since, Ekaterina Sergeyevna Tsevetayeva, mistress of Marston Mauditt, Sir Jakub Haven's lady and mine.

45

12 There were three scientists working with Sir Jakub Haven at Marston Mauditt. The only Englishman was called Daniel Roscoe, a scraggy beanpole of a man with a prominent Adam's apple who dressed in an old greengage-coloured sports jacket and the brown corduroy trousers that were then fashionable. He had a lean, lugubrious face, a long querulous nose, and sad eyes. His father was a Durham shipwright and his uncles were all miners. He had made his way entirely on scholarships as you always could if you were that good. The ladder of opportunity, as some education-alist rightly said, was narrow and steeply raked; but it was always there. Daniel had taken it. He was, according to Leila who had it from her father, the most brilliant physicist of his generation, though then only just turned thirty.

The second was H. O. Bahadur, who had come from New Delhi to study under Haven at Cambridge, and had won his spurs in the Cavendish Laboratory. He was younger, naturally exotic, and immensely rich. I'm not sure he wasn't royal. At any rate he smoked Havana cigars, drank Dom Perignon like lemon-ade, had hampers of food sent down from Fortnum's, and went to the races whenever possible. He lived at our local pub, The Pitcher of Good Ale, where he amazed and scandalised the locals by his assaults on the modesty of the village girls. We discovered later that he had a wife and several children back home. He spoke an English that had not been uttered in this country since the death of Edward VII.

The third scientist was an American called Ed Ashburn. He was the only one to have a wife with him. Ed and Dottie were Anglophiles of a particularly ferocious kind. They had felt the disease coming on before they had even arrived, and once they had settled into a somewhat mildewed cottage on the estate, they were hopeless addicts. Ed could have doubled for Bing Crosby, while Dottie was Judy Garland without the voice.

'We think the cottage is just darling,' Dottie told us after they had made their first inspection.

'Just swell after Los Angeles,' Ed confirmed.

I could never quite determine whether Ed really was a simpleton, with a hole in his head into which his Maker had absentmindedly poured the Quantum Theory, or whether his total performance while he lived at Marston Mauditt was one enormous confidence trick. If so, he was a consummate jester.

What I do know is that the Ashburns, in their singleminded determination to be more English than the English, nearly drove my long-suffering grandfather off his rocker. He was ready to forgive the gnomes they planted in their own patch of garden, but the maypole on the croquet lawn outside the windows of the big house was too much, and their clod-hopping attempts at a Morris dance there on midsummer day, which churned his beautiful grass into a quagmire, temporarily deranged him. Frankly, if the Ashburns had been starting school right now, they'd have been classified as educationally subnormal. I'm told many mathematicians and physicists of high achievement grow lop-sided in this way, their brains put out of synch by the weight of their gifts.

13 In the summer of 1946 I had some leave due, and Leila wrote suggesting that we should meet in Finland to see what had happened to her parents' house. It seemed a splendid notion, for I'd heard so much about the house at Metsäpirrti that I felt I'd been there already. So I hitched a ride into Hamburg, and caught the next boat to Helsinki. Leila was waiting at the quayside with an old Mercedes-Benz that a friend of her father's, the Finnish mathematician Professor Helstrom, had lent us.

I watched her from the ship as we tied up, caught in that curious panic which grips you at the sight of a loved face after absence. There is a moment when the memory loses its foothold and is uncertain whether to signal friend or foe. We seem to know that there is a lover inside that stranger's body; or is it a stranger inside that lover? I had never been so close to any human being as to Leila; but what if the space that still remained between us was in truth limitless? Why should I love this woman on the quayside with the glint of Chablis in her hair and the astonishing green eyes and the conspirator's grin, and not some other woman? She waved and the doubt dissolved in an unbidden surge of straight happiness. It was going to be all right, at any rate, for this snatched piece of time.

'Well, Ben, darling, we made it,' she said between the kisses. 'We made it to Metsäpirrti.'

She drove out of Helsinki. The spring comes late there, but when it does, it brings with it an unparalleled sense of release, and all those strange, bottled-up people whose ancestors once unaccountably trekked north from Hungary seem to uncoil in the sun. We drove east towards the Russian border through lush acres of pine trees and along unending lakes. Leila turned on the radio and picked up the American Band of the AEF playing *Frenesi*; then eased the Mercedes up to 120 kilometres. It was

48

one of those moments when, if the car had spun off the road and killed us both instantly, it would have seemed perfectly all right.

We came across the house quite suddenly. We'd been winding down a lane for a mile or more and then there it was just as she'd described it, in a clearing of the forest, the great lake behind it now unfrozen and glinting in the spring sunshine, its wooden shutters all closed as if to conceal some secret life. But there was life in the kitchen; Leila knocked and the old man Matti, their factotum at Metsäpirrti, emerged, blinking against the light and then beaming with delight at the sight of Leila. They embraced like father and daughter, and Matti called for his wife Kirstie to come. This good old soul came shuffling out, at first cross, then bemused, and finally as transported as her husband. They talked in Finnish, a soft but totally incomprehensible language, and then Leila disentangled herself and laughing, introduced me. 'Heh heh,' I exclaimed weakly. It was the only greeting I knew, but it seemed to go down well enough. We went into the kitchen, and seated round the table over a celebratory vodka, they told their story.

It seemed that after the fall of Finland in the heroic Hundred Days War the house had been occupied by Russian officers, who had behaved quite correctly. Then when the Germans came, they'd had German officers, who'd also been correct, though not so *sympathique*. I discovered to my surprise that, though the Finns had fought in their history some seventy or eighty wars against the Russians, they still had little or no rancour against the ordinary Russian man or woman, whom they considered cousins. As for the German alliance, well, that had been caused by the necessities of history; it didn't oblige them actually to like the Germans.

And then of course the Russians had stormed back into Karelia, and they'd had them back again. The fighting had been much further north and the house had been spared. They undid the front door and let us in.

It was precisely as I'd imagined; and it remains one of my two or three favourite houses in the world. It was timbered and double-glazed against the Finnish winter and what we now call open plan. The windows of the dining room looked out over the lake, and on the first floor there was a huge lumber room that had been turned into a casual library. A corridor ran right down one side leading to the bedrooms; each had a name painted in

Finnish on its door. We explored the house like children, hand in hand, while the old couple beamed approvingly. The marks of alien occupation were few and far between; Matti had painted the scuff marks over and Kirstie had spring-cleaned.

'The sauna,' Leila remembered suddenly. 'Did they spoil the sauna?' We dashed downstairs and down the path to the wooden shed by the lake where it was housed. Inside it was spotless — and baking hot. 'Marvellous!' Leila cried. 'We'll have one now; I haven't felt really clean since we left Finland.' Matti and Kirstie discreetly withdrew to make a celebratory supper, and we threw off our clothes. I found the dry heat curiously soothing. Soon the globules of sweat began to run down our bodies. She was right; whatever else it was, it wasn't a sexual experience. She got up and ladled another pailful of cool green water onto the stove. It hissed and steamed alarmingly and the temperature rose perceptibly. 'Now for that famous beating, Ben,' she said. She picked up a handful of birch leaves and slapped them playfully over me. If this is flagellation, I thought, give me more. We grew lobster-pink; the hot air seemed to singe the nostrils and I began to wilt. 'Time to cool off, Ben,' she advised. She opened the door, ran through the shed and down the jetty which stretched out to the lake. Then with a neat dive she was in that icy water. I hesitated, then plunged after her. After the first shock, when I thought my heart had stopped, the water was delicious. We swam and splashed, then had another go at the sauna, another swim, a shower, a hard towelling, then lay back on the wooden benches and drank cold bottled beer which Matti had thoughtfully left there. I felt newborn, and told her so. She laughed. 'You're one of us now, Ben,' she assured me.

That evening we had dinner looking over the lake, the table lit by a dozen or more fat crimson candles. We had caviare, and then their summer speciality, crayfish, and then a dish of sybaritic shamelessness — a soufflé laced with farm cream. The Germans had thoughtfully left some twelve dozen bottles of plundered Burgundy in the cellar, so we helped ourselves to a magnificent Puligny-Montrachet. Matti produced some cognac and cigars and we settled round the log fire, for even in mid-summer, the nights were chilly in that latitude. Leila searched through the records and put on an old Duke Ellington classic called *Solitude* — the one he wrote in twenty minutes back in

1934 to fill out a record in a session. Matti and Kirstie said they must go to bed and kissed us goodnight as if we really were their children. We lay in front of the fire half asleep and, in one of those moments that come only half a dozen times in a life, to us, Time, that world champion gooseberry, made his excuses and left the room.

So by definition I don't know how long we were there before the telephone rang. Leila swore and picked it up resignedly. I watched her face cloud with some private care as she listened. Then she answered curtly and put the receiver down rather unnecessarily hard. I looked at her enquiringly. 'Just an old friend of my parents saying hello,' she explained.

I couldn't help reflecting that she had been unusually brusque in the face of such innocent benevolence. There was something else: my knowledge of Finnish was limited to *heh heh*; but around the kitchen at Marston Mauditt I'd picked up enough Russian to know when someone says in that language that they're busy and can't talk now.

14 There was one uneasy problem I'd been made to face: How would Sue and Leila react to each other? What was between Sue and myself was not important, at least not particularly to me, or so I liked to think; but I'd been taught that one didn't just ditch people, and even today I suppose that holds good whatever else has changed. So one didn't just ditch Sue — who in any event was not wholly mine to ditch — but what then precisely did one do? The dilemma — if that is what it was — quickly dissolved. Soon after we met I introduced Leila to Sue at The Pitcher of Good Ale on market day in Marston Mauditt, and they at once became locked in a dialectic, a code if you like, to which I still haven't found the key. They became inseparable. If you tried to eavesdrop on a snatch of their talk, it sounded pretty banal, being taken up, as far as I could see, with what was going in the local shops; nevertheless, I got the impression that some deeper level of communication was going on between them underneath the literal one.

Sue completed her secretarial course around this time and went off to a job at the BBC. Here she soon became involved in a torrid affair with a man called Nigel Turret-Smith, a bald-headed coot old enough to be her father, and one of the biggest twats it has ever been my misfortune to meet. What she saw in him totally escapes me; but then to tell the truth one can never see what one's friends see in the people with whom they mate. Nigel tormented and delighted her for some seven or more months, when he obligingly settled the matter by dying of coronary thrombosis when they were in bed together. Mrs. Turret-Smith, the inevitable harridan waiting in the wings, took it amiss. As I've said, Sue was one of the world's losers, but none the less lovable for that.

It might be assumed from this sad chronicle that Sue had dismissed me from her mind. This was not the case. One day in

1947, by one of those fortunate conjunctions which occur to the world's seducers just so often, I was home on leave and Leila was away with her father in Paris at an international conference on the peaceful uses of atomic energy. It was one of the few genuinely warm days in that ghastly year, and the morning she rang the entire animal creation seemed to murmur with lust. The system was that at the cottage we had an extension from the big house, which was always switched through when they were away. Sue called, at her most biddable, and invited me round for a swim. It was a Saturday, and her own parents were away at the caravan. I went, having nothing better to do. Sue greeted me in a lascivious white bathing wrap. Her father had built a swimming pool from his ill-gotten gains below his vegetable garden, and we were soon splashing around in it noisily. We stayed in so long that the skin on our fingers began to wrinkle from the water; we felt extended and clean. Then we lay side by side on our stomachs and sunbathed by the pool. She was wearing a two-piece costume which only just accommodated her, and what with Sue and the sun and the water and the exercise, I soon felt deliciously and unreservedly randy. The blood was pounding into my loins for all the world like some God-invented hydraulic jack, lifting my hips clear of the ground, and I instinctively put out my hand towards her, my eyes closed against the sun. She took it, and dug her nails into my palm. I rolled over towards her, but she wriggled free and, to my intense surprise, peeled off her top, revealing her delectable tits to the caressing summer air, then dived into the pool. It worked. I jumped up and dived in after her, cleaving through the water to where she hovered like some shimmering salmon trout. We touched, grappled, surfaced, gasping for air and spraying drops of water in stroboscopic profusion. Then we began one of those half-serious, half-joking wrestling rapes, in which both sides acquiesce but feign force. We splashed, heaved and turned in Joe Carter's multi-gallon waterbed. I got the bottom half of her bikini down to her thighs while she prettily feigned a resistance that did not chime logically with the proprietary hand she had deep in my crotch, and then we were both gloriously free of all encumbrance and at it in the water; a feat perfectly possible, for those who haven't yet tried it, given will, lust, knack and luck.

53

15 I joined the army when I was nineteen and, as Toby feared, had a very quiet war. By the time my basic square-bashing and interpreter's course were over, both VE and VJ days had come with their false dawns and, after briefly lighting our skies with their splendour, had left us all to struggle with rebuilding the ruins of Europe. I spent some time in Germany working as an extremely junior intelligence officer and saw enough to convince myself that whatever price Germany had inflicted on Europe had been paid back in full measure, if you wanted to see the total catastrophe in terms of primal vengeance. I shall never forget my first experience of France, where I had to go first to join my unit. Here was a country beaten flat, bled dry, embittered by the nightmare of occupation. And yet, and yet. When our troop train stopped at dawn that first morning in France, we pulled up the blinds to see that we had come to a clearing where the French were going to give us breakfast. Dozens of women with brawny arms and businesslike aprons swarmed round the trestle tables and a divine aroma of freshly made coffee pervaded the air. There was bread straight from the oven, and butter straight from the farm, and splendid dishes of *oeufs brouillés*, a simple meal which we, the victors, had not tasted in six years of war. I suppose in a sense we should have realised then that the real winners were our hosts that morning, and that Germany, too, having failed to beat us in the lunacy of hot war, would do so soon in the jousting ground of capitalist peace. After all, like diplomacy, it's only an extension of war by other means.

16 My parents didn't like Leila but then she didn't like them and I frankly couldn't stand them. They came back from India to Attlee's England in 1946 with evident reluctance and took a flat of monumental tastelessness off Baker Street. Quite apart from the natural gap that must grow between people six years and six thousand miles apart, I found that we now spoke a totally different language. My father had become a director of one of those giant Anglo-American international companies and had made a killing with them. Now he was on leave of absence while he decided what to do next. I had expected to find him older but not mottled by cirrhosis of the liver; I knew he had gone away a snob and a conservative, but had not expected to find him return a fascist and racist. He boasted that he had blunted his razor throwing it at his servant. It did not take him long to decide that Southern Rhodesia was the best place for him and I daresay he was right. My mother seemed to have desiccated in the sun; she did nothing but talk nostalgically of her life as a mem-sahib and go to the hairdressers. They were refugees from the twentieth century. I saw them off at Waterloo station one day in 1947 with a distinct sense of relief, and yet, once they had gone, I felt a most unwelcome access of loneliness, for my grandparents were now getting on and I'd somehow vaguely assumed my parents would come back and take up their traditional roles again. I had Leila but I didn't own her, and I wanted too much perhaps to possess, and be possessed. In my melancholy I took the next train to Marston Mauditt, and went to seek out my grandfather in his workshop. It was a room I loved, with its solid level surface, well-kept tools, and perennial smell of wood shavings. I always admired his dexterity, having inherited none of it, especially since I suspected that, had he not come from a long line of Wiltshire farmworkers and cabinet makers and wheel-wrights,

but had the opportunities of Sir Jakub Haven, he might have ended up holding his own with him in some Senior Common Room. As it was, the Professor had discovered something Taverstock had not in all their years together; that he was employing an extremely useful chess player as his bailiff. So after that the two of them would while away many a pleasant evening playing together. The truth was, they had simply become friends.

William Freeman was working at his bench when I put my head round the door, but he stopped at once; since he had no more rapport with his son than I had, it made our own accord the closer. Their one embarrassed meeting, when my father came down in his hired Bentley, was even more excruciating than mine had been.

'Well, boy, they've gone, have they?'

'Yes, I saw them off just an hour ago.'

'Ah well.' He picked up a tool absentmindedly. 'They'll be better off there.'

'I daresay.'

'And how about you, young Ben? Will you miss them?'

'Frankly no. I think of this as home now.'

'Good.'

'And I've got Leila.'

'Yes.' He examined some non-existent defect in his plans.

'What do you think of her?'

'Leila?' He was buying time. 'She's a bright little girl. Her dad's very proud of her.'

'Yes, I know that. But how do you think of her yourself?'

He hesitated again. 'Well, Ben, I think she's just fine for the moment. Good — er — experience for you.'

'No more?'

'That's not for me to say, boy. Except you're both very young.'

'Yes, of course. I mean, she doesn't take it seriously at all.'

'That's what I was meaning to say, boy. There's a certain kind of woman, always has been, that's very good for a young chap but not to be taken seriously if you follow me. No, never seriously.'

He picked up his plane and made an absentminded adjustment to it.

I should have much liked to pursue the conversation. For

56

instance, was it possible that some such turbulent enchantress had once enlivened the young days of this now serene and wise old man? It would have been fascinating to know, but impossible to ask. There was a silence.

'She'll be trouble, Ben,' he suddenly said. 'I don't mean she'll want to do harm, for she has great qualities; she's honest, and truthful, and straight. And she has a good heart. Yes, I truly think she has a good heart.' He was released from his own inhibitions now, surprised by his own unexpected candour. 'And there's no side to her. Not an inch. No. In fact, I can't truthfully put my finger on it.' He paused again.

'You just feel it?'

'That's it. Or shall we say this: I think I've known someone a bit like that years ago.'

I waited for him to go on. But he was miles away, years away, and I was delighted to see a slow grin creep over his weather-beaten face. 'That was before your grandmother, of course, Ben. Long before that. And I don't regret it. Not one little bit. Only I had enough sense to get out in time.' He was looking straight at me now, and we were sharing a secret that had long been buried. I was thoroughly diverted by this unexpected confidence.

'So it's all right, as long as I treat it strictly as a — sort of joke?'

He nodded. 'A lot of things in life are best treated that way, if only we could see it.'

'I think she sees it as a bit of a joke.'

'I'm sure she does, boy. But can you?'

'I think so. I'll have to.'

'Yes.' With unexpected affirmation in his voice: 'You must, Ben.'

17 The only other event that mattered in 1947 was Toby's twenty-first. His parents, Hannibal and Marjorie, (it was hard to see how the poor clod could have done much anyway with a start like that) had their drawbacks, but meanness wasn't one of them. There were two hundred guests, a marquee on the lawn, two bands, and champagne all night. It was the first really grand do I'd been to; and my natural diffidence was greatly compounded by an absurd worry about whom to take. I loved Leila; Sue was to the world's eyes my girl; it was not the sort of problem that should really have detained me a moment. Toby settled it by asking Sue to be his partner. I agreed with a mock struggle, and the four of us had dinner together before the mighty piss-up began. Toby was in his number one uniform, as I suppose befitted a regular naval officer; I was in an ill-fitting dinner jacket hired for the occasion; Leila wore black with stunning effect; Sue was in a pink dress that was a dreadful mistake from the word go. It was, I think, the first and last occasion I've ever attended where the girls carried a *carnet de bal*. My inclination was to book Leila solid, but reason and manners prevailed. I left a couple of spots for Toby and one for his father.

It was a night that still returns in my dreams. The band played *Oh, What A Beautiful Mornin'* and *I Get A Kick Out of You* and *La Mer* and *South Rampart Street Parade*. There was cold lobster for supper and eggs and bacon at dawn. I gradually grew rather lightheaded with the excitement and the drink, and had to put my head under the cold tap in our cottage at one stage. I danced with Leila till Toby's number came up in her dance card, and with some reluctance handed her over to him and escorted Sue onto the floor. Leila danced as she made love, with a natural and instinctive grace; with joy. Sue danced — and screwed — with great gusto but little sense of rhythm. After we'd been round the floor a half a dozen times or so I suggested we sit out for a while.

Sue accepted, no doubt thinking I had some romantic motive. Sue always thought like that. We strolled along the Henderson's garden path, away from the dancing, through the rose garden and across the croquet lawn. The White House glittered in the spotlights as if it were made out of sugar icing. The band were playing *Blue Skies* and it was nearly three in the morning. The first tentative pale fingers of a midsummer English dawn were caught in the sky like a thief with his hand in the till. Sue squeezed my hand and seemed to be towing me gently in the direction of the Henderson's summer-house, a Victorian folly that stood on the edge of the croquet lawn. But if we wanted it to ourselves we were too late. A few feet short, Sue stopped. There were two figures just discernible through the glass door. One, I realised at once, was Toby. The uniform was unmistakable. He lay back in the chaise-longue that the Hendersons still affected, while a girl lay with her head in his lap. And then, as the first fireworks whooshed into the sky, I saw quite clearly that it was Leila. Toby's white face was momentarily illumined in the exploding multi-coloured glare of the rockets and I saw his mouth half open as if he were crying out; and I thought that he looked just as I must have done on the day of my initiation in Leila's room.

18 Next day I woke feeling like a tube of toothpaste that has come to the end of its working life. It was not just the pain in my head from the champagne but the pain in my heart at the memory of the scene in the summerhouse. I lay back in my bed and tried to rationalise it away, but it wouldn't go. It didn't matter, Leila didn't matter, I was a man of the world, one simply had to laugh these things off. No dice. Finally I rolled out of bed. Rosanna was busy in the kitchen: the clock said eleven.

'Good morning, Ben. Would you like some breakfast?'

'Thanks, Granma, I couldn't. But I'd love some coffee.'

'Too much to drink, I daresay.'

'Not really. Sick at heart. Jealous.'

'Ah.' She had her back to me, but I could feel her quickening interest. 'Leila's been upsetting you.'

'Yes.'

'You don't own her, Ben.'

'I know.'

'Here's your coffee.'

'You're an angel.'

She was too. She sat opposite me, her still beautiful face full of gentle concern.

'You're very young, Ben.'

'I can't help it.'

'I mean — she's much older than you in her ways.'

'Too true.'

'You'll be the one to be hurt.'

'I'm hurt now.'

'Forget her, Ben. Sue's the girl for you.'

'She's not interested in me. She's got a new bloke in London.'

'Pah!' She made a sour face. 'That's nothing. All young girls go through that sort of thing. Just because he seems mature and sophisticated. She prefers you really.'

'I like Sue. Always did. Always will. But Leila fascinates me.'

She sighed. 'It'll pass, Ben. It always does.'

'You sound as if you know.'

'I do.'

I studied her with renewed interest. Like most young people, I liked to delude myself that the torments and delights of sexual passion had been invented by my own generation; that in all previous ages the thing was done as a sort of clockwork duty. For a moment my imagination boiled and a whole series of pornographic frames starring Rosanna and William *en amoureux* flashed through my horrified mind before the internal censor cancelled them. I shook myself to clear the forbidden memory. Rosanna beamed at me, innocent of what had just happened inside my head, or so I like to think. 'Cheer up, Ben,' she said. 'You'll get over it.'

I kissed her and wandered out of the cottage. My idea was to avoid Leila that day, and go back to my unit early on Monday. That would give the grievous wound time to heal, and by the time I came back on leave again, Leila would be forgotten. That at any rate was the plan.

It didn't work. Driven by some subconscious force I could not control, I found myself walking along the side of the lake. I had not gone more than thirty paces when I saw Leila walking towards me.

I could of course have turned and hurried away, but that would have seemed infantile. So I walked on po-faced, watching her gamine grin of pleasure as she saw me.

'Good morning, Leila,' I said stiffly as we drew near, and tried to walk by.

'Hey, wait a minute.' She was close and frowning now, and in the morning sun she seemed to glow with health like a gravure advertisement. 'What's the matter with you, young Ben?'

'Nothing.' I was useless at this sort of thing.

'Nothing nuts.' She came close, and I felt my will liquidising as if it had been put in a high-speed mixer. 'You're cross, Ben. You're on your dignity. It doesn't suit you. In fact it makes you look rather ridiculous.'

'I daresay it does.' I made as if to pass her.

'Not too fast.' She was genuinely puzzled now. 'Have I done something to upset you?'

'Certainly not. If you want to carry on a shoddy affair with Toby, go ahead. I don't give a damn.'

She frowned a moment longer, then burst into peals of laughter.

'Ben, you're priceless. What on earth did you think we were doing in the summer-house?'

'What you do in the summer-house with Toby is your business. I just didn't think it very — ah — dignified.'

She was walking beside me now, mock serious, arm linked in mine, head solemnly lowered. We paced along in silence a bit.

'Let me tell you two things, Ben,' she said at last. 'First, if I wanted a quick affair with Toby, I'd have one, and nobody in the whole world could stop me.'

'No, I'm sure they couldn't. I just think you might show a little more taste.'

'Taste, is it?' She stopped and turned quickly to face me. 'Toby may not be everybody's cup of tea. As it happens, he certainly isn't mine. But he will damn certainly be somebody's. That's how the world goes round, Ben. And talking of taste, did I ever say I minded about Sue?'

'That's different.' But I was uneasy. It had suddenly dawned on me that whether or not Leila and Toby had actually been at it in the summer-house, I had certainly been at it with Sue in her father's pool. But that was utterly different; a moment of madness, a mindless folly, a sly trick by the goddess of all amorous conjunctions.

'Come on, Ben,' she said. 'Let's go for a drive and talk.' We strolled round to the garage and found her father's car invitingly at hand. She took the wheel then and always: I'm a lousy driver, while she was fast but sure. She headed towards Selborne, the place where an obscure clergyman called Gilbert White kept a diary some forty years on the local wildlife that was to make him unwittingly immortal. The village was largely unchanged, and the view from the Hanger must have been, save for the odd telegraph wire, just as he'd seen it when he and his brother had finished cutting the zig-zag path to the top. When you get up there and sit beneath the beeches, there's a gentle soughing breeze but otherwise perfect stillness, and in this pool of quietness you can hear the yammer of your useless thoughts dissolving until you're at one with creation. There was a wishing stone, but by that time you didn't really have anything to wish for. We sat down by it, nevertheless. I felt much better and decided it was up to me to make amends.

'I'm sorry I was such a pompous twit. I can't explain it.'

'Never apologise and never explain.'

In my new, mature man-of-the-world persona, I rather liked that, even though I was vaguely aware that I'd heard it before somewhere. I chewed it over a bit.

'Yes, I suppose that is your philosophy.'

'That's rather overdoing it. Let's call it my thought for the day.'

'It just seemed so — out of keeping with everything we'd done and said.'

She grinned, opening one eye at me.

'And what had we done that said I shouldn't do what you thought I did?'

'There are some things that don't need saying when two people are as close as us.'

'And there are apparently some that do.'

I waited. She frowned, concentrating.

'The first is that I love you, Ben, very much, idiot that you are; more than you can understand. The second is that this love belongs to here and now. It can't be taken away or cancelled or diminished, just as our being on this hill here and now can't be taken away or cancelled or diminished. Whatever happens, it stands. Love once found can be forgotten or discarded but not lost. It's safe, and unchanging.'

'You mean that it's as if the clock has stopped.'

'If you like, yes. As if we had stopped the clock.'

'If only we could.'

'We can.'

'What marvellous arrogance.'

'It's not we who are arrogant but time. Time's lost without an audience. He won't appear unless he's top of the bill. Take away his applause, he just curls up and dies.'

'What about the past?'

'I reckon that the past is a dream.'

'And the future?'

'The future is' — she sought the right word — 'an illusion.'

'And the present?'

63

'The present, Ben,' — and here she kissed me tenderly — 'is a joke. A very good joke, which is to be thoroughly enjoyed, even by solemn twits like you.'

'I've never met anyone remotely like you.'

'There are plenty of people remotely like me. But there's no one exactly like me. I'm myself, and don't ever forget it. I'm unique, and independent and sovereign. I own nobody, and nobody owns me.'

'It sounds a pretty reckless doctrine to me.'

She hesitated, then said, 'There was a man once for whom I'd have done anything; but I think he's dead.'

I must have looked crestfallen, because she said,

'Don't be so melancholy, Ben. You don't know what heartache I've saved you today.'

'You mean by shattering my dreams before they shatter me.'

'By trying to show you the seduction of simple truth.'

'Truth is never simple.'

'*You* want to teach me that!'

'I don't want to teach you anything. I only want to be allowed to love you.'

She laughed a lot at that.

'Granted. And now, Ben, I want to give you something. Something solid and precious to celebrate and fix in your mind this exact moment.' She reached for her bag and took out a small blue box. 'I'd meant to give you this today anyway, but our talk gives it extra point.' She opened the box and took out a curious gold signet ring made in segments which you could just discern. It was very old, and it had some sign engraved on it in a script I did not understand.

'This, Ben, is called the Enigma Ring. It was given to my father's grandfather who was a doctor at the Russian court. It was for saving the life of one of the royal princes. He always said the boy would have recovered anyway, but that's as maybe. It was handed down to my father, and he's given it to me. It's the most precious thing we possess. If you lose it, you get bad luck and all that crap. If you can open it, that proves you have the key to happiness. Here, I'll show you.'

She took it apart, and it looked simple. She put it together and handed it to me. It was curiously heavy and very smooth. I didn't want to let it go. It had the strange, comforting texture

64

of a worry stone. Try as I would though, I couldn't put it together. She laughed. 'Let me show you again.'

She did, and again I failed to follow her legerdemain.

'I don't seem to have the key to happiness.'

'You'll learn. Keep it, Ben, to make this day distinct and unique and to give you certain proof when you doubt that today I loved you.'

'But I can't possibly keep anything as valuable as this.'

'You possibly can. It'll do you good to have the responsibility. It'll do you good to remember every time you look at it how much somebody cared about you.'

'But your father — '

' "It was my turquoise. I had it of Leah when I was a bachelor. I would not have given it for a wilderness of monkeys." But my father isn't Shylock. And my mother isn't Leah. And I'm not Jessica. Keep it so long as you love me.'

'You're giving it to me for ever?'

'If you love me that long, well and good.' It was comforting on my little finger. I pondered.

'What you're really saying is that you'd give me anything.'

'Anything that's mine to give.'

'Except a sovereign, independent island called Leila.'

'You may visit, and you might be asked to stay. But no, you can't own me. That's just greedy.'

I pondered some more, then said:

'In that case, there's only one thing more to be said.'

'And what's that, Ben?'

'Thank you.'

She laughed. 'Ben you've done something I thought no one could ever do.'

'What's that?'

'You've made me feel a little ashamed.'

19 Daniel and I sat by the lake one day that summer and unexpectedly he began to talk. I'd just been reading Zola's *Germinal*, and was much absorbed by the miner's life. Daniel told me that though his father was a shipwright, and a good one, all his uncles were miners. Except that few in the north-east used the word miner; they were pitmen. All his uncles, and of course his father too, looked forward to the day when the state took over the mines; they had suffered too much too long; first the humiliation of the 1921 strike that failed, and then the dreadful memory of the General Strike of 1926 when everyone had gone back to work by mid-May except the miners; hunger drove them back to work six months later. Daniel talked with a little smile on his sad face of the great miners' gala at Durham when they took over the town and the greatest men of the left in the land came north to speak to them and there were great marches with the banners of each lodge proudly carried. It was a male world where father was boss and the women busied themselves over their bubbling pots and pans; since the war, the real value of coal had at last become starkly clear; one young man in ten was sent down the mines to hew coal instead of kill Germans, and at last the wage at the coal face rose to a respectable sum; ten or even fifteen pounds. Great and generous hosts, the miners now kept ample table for themselves and their friends; they raced pigeons and whippets; and they drank gallons of beer for their thirst's sake and their soul's comfort. They spoke two languages, these separate and proud men; a profane patois for the coalface and a carefully correct version for the home; they never swore in front of their families. They had their own clubs, where a local lad would get up and sing a song or two, the progenitors of those great rafts of prosperity they run today which are in effect an extension of international showbusiness. He talked, and I let him talk, for to me as

66

a bourgeois southron, it was a fabled place I had never seen and could not understand; and it's this yawning gap in our comprehension of one another which is surely at the root of our problems still today. Daniel said he would concede that there were entrepreneurs who had contributed their brains and their energies to certain industries; but for the mine-owners he had nothing but contempt. They had never contributed anything, he said, except their greed, and indifference, and stupidity.

20 I remember another day that summer when Leila and I followed the river two miles downstream to where it flows into the limpid waters of the Meon and lay under a willow tree making gentle, sun-dappled love. I confess gladly — and may not be unique in it — that though there are some moments of splendour to recall in my life, a handful of triumphs winnowed by merciful memory out of all the defeats, an odd alpha minus or hit for six, nothing means quite so much as that tender alfresco fuck in the fragrant summer grass.

We lay there afterwards, staring up through the branches at the unshockable sky. I had a tiresome question to ask.

'Leila, do you believe in God?'

She picked a straw and sucked it rather unhygienically. Then she smiled.

'Dear Ben, what a holy fool you are!'

'I suppose I must seem a bit of a twit.'

'Don't be depressed. You are a particularly charming twit.'

'You don't have to answer.'

'You didn't have to ask. But you have. So I shall try but it's not easy.' She frowned and chewed her straw.

'Of course not — if you mean that mad old sadist the Jews used to haggle with in Israel. But I believe in gods.'

·'Pagan gods?'

'Yes. I think they're everywhere.'

'Turn but a stone and start a wing.'

'Yes, that sort of thing. Or to put it another way — they're a convenient explanation for what lies on the other side of the physical world.'

'You think there is something?'

'I'm sure of it. You know what my father's friends are now working on? It's a most extraordinary idea — that there's a whole mirror world existing in the reflection of our known, literal world.'

'Are they really? Christ, how spooky.'

'Exactly. That's why the gods are such a comfort. They're mirror images of us. Greedy, jealous, sexy, fallible. Lovable.'

'Do you believe in love?'

She grinned broadly. There was a little rash of freckles over her nose and her cheekbones.

'Really, Ben, you are priceless.'

'Then you must forgive me. You see, I've always been looking for a woman more intelligent than myself who could explain things to me.'

At this naive confession she burst into peals of laughter. Finally, she had to wipe the tears from her eyes with her handkerchief. I looked on, vaguely mystified, then tried lamely to explain.

'And somehow, I thought you were the one.'

She sighed, and looked down into her crumpled handkerchief for a moment.

'I'll tell you what, Ben — I believe in making love.'

'With anybody?'

'No, idiot, not with anybody. Uniquely, specially and specifically with somebody.'

'Somebody like me?'

She nodded solemnly. 'Pretty much like you, Ben.'

And that, I thought, was that. The next morning though, as I lay sleeping in that voluptuary's bed in the cottage, my grandfather already an hour or more into his day's labours, my grandmother already gone to her domestic cares in the big house, Leila stole in through our open back door and tip-toed up the stairs, took off her cotton dress and crept in beside me so quietly that I could not be sure if she wasn't part of that customary early morning dream of lust which visits most young men. She kissed me awake, put my hand where it belonged, and whispered in my ear:

'Ben, I wasn't very nice to you yesterday. I want you to know the truth because I care for you enough to trouble you with it. I believe in making love. In fact I love it. And I suddenly realised

69

this morning how much I love making love with you. Yes, Ben, like that. Yes. And I — '

But whatever else she wanted to tell me, she decided not to tell me then; or on second thoughts, perhaps she did, though not in so many words.

21 Leila's father, Sir Jakub Haven, was, I suppose, at this time fifty years old, a short broad man with silver hair, thick spectacles and one of those wide Central European noses. I learned later that he had worked his way through University at Prague and later at Vienna as you could in those days when fees were low and living cheap; his own father had been a kosher butcher somewhere in Moravia and he was one of five boys. His eldest brother Isaac emigrated to California and was teaching philosophy at UCLA; the second brother Reuben was in New York, and had made a great deal of money on the commodity market. Jakub was the third brother; Saul, the fourth, the problem child of the family, had drifted pretty aimlessly until Hitler came in 1938, when Jakub brought him to England; now he ran a small hotel on the south coast with money Jakub had lent him. Bruno, the youngest, had been a lawyer in Vienna and an ardent communist; he'd gone underground when the Germans came and had not been heard of since. The Nobel Prize was worth £20,000 in those days; I suppose you could add a nought for the present value, and it was from this treasure trove that the finance for Saul had come. I looked up Haven's achievements in a book on Nobel Prize-winners once but could make little sense of it; it seemed to have something to do with uranium 235.

Professor Haven had most of the qualities of a Central European bourgeois of his generation; he was first, a formidable paterfamilias. No detail of his daughter's life, nor his wife's, was too minor to escape his scrupulous attention. This, while a boon to a woman of his wife's generation, was nerve-racking for someone who was not, like Leila. Father and daughter were too similar. Sometimes, when I got to know them better, I was present when they had shattering, volcanic rows with tears and cries on both sides and unforgivable insults cannonading to and fro like mortar-fire; then all would be calm again and the injuries forgiven if not forgotten. They loved each other well enough, after their fashion.

He spoke English to the end of his days passably, but with a thick accent which could sometimes be comic. Once, when he heard that I had taken up rowing as a little light relief from exams at school he told me that a distinguished Oxford colleague had taken him to the Boat Races: 'He was as student der little fellow who steers; how do you call him? Der cock I think.' When he said 'How much' it sounded like 'How mech?' and when he said 'Bag' it came out like 'buck', so that when, standing in front of the fire, he passed round the cigarettes, asking his guests if anyone would like a fag, Leila used to fall about with laughter.

Not surprisingly perhaps, he was a pessimist in politics, and was disenchanted with revolution, though like most young men born in his time and place, he had been a communist for a short while till he came face-to-face with its gritty imperatives.

He enjoyed entertaining, and even in wartime his table seemed never to want, though in retrospect I think this was only partly because we lived in the country and could always rely on the farm for basics: they just had a knack of making food go further and taste better. It was as their frequent guest that I quickly acquired a lifelong love of rollmops and sauerkraut, chopped liver, loks, garlic, dill pickles, borscht, and kvass. He drank very little, a thimbleful of whisky to be sociable or a sip of champagne to celebrate. He loved the theatre and the opera but could never have succeeded at either as he had once hoped; though his voice was generous he had no sense of pitch. He was an ardent anglophile, and an agnostic who had discarded the nominal religion of his fathers while yielding not an iota of their *Weltanschauung*. He remained a quintessential Jew. He suffered long black periods of melancholy when he was struggling with some new piece of theoretical work, and would pace along beside the lake for hours at a time lost in the mind-racked reverie of the creative scientist; then he would go to his study and work late into the night; sometimes my grandmother would go in at six in the morning and find him asleep in the big armchair, his log fire a pile of grey ash; beside him a sheaf of papers covered in mathematical symbols. All he needed to work, indeed, was paper and pencil, though there was a small laboratory later in one of the outhouses where his scientists could do practical experiments.

He was the first great man I ever met; and because of his eminence, great, or at least interesting men came to his house. Professor Lindemann swept down one day in a government Humber; once Haven was summoned to Chequers to see Winston; the police kept a special watch on him and Inspector Tripp used to drop in once a week, ostensibly to see that all was well but in fact to have a large free whisky. Jakub Haven in short brought a scent of cosmopolitan glamour to our bucolic little community, but was not always understood all the same.

22 On Christmas Eve 1947 the Havens gave a party with a tree and presents. We sat, servants, scientists and all, around the dining room table a whit bemused and ate one of our farm turkeys with all the right trimmings and a splendid pudding which my grandmother had made. A fair measure of vodka went round and then Kitty announced that we should have some entertainment. This was, of course, long before television had replaced the parlour game and so that night she decided we should make our own amusement. No one had to perform, but anyone could who so wished. First Leila played for us; dreamy pieces of Chopin and then, for me I think, the slow movement of the *Pathétique* and then, for her father, *Plaisir d'Amour*. There was polite applause.

'Come now, Ben,' Kitty encouraged me, 'I'm sure you can do something. You're a clever boy.'

I rose to my feet and recited Gautier's *Symphonie en Blanc Majeur*, feeling an utter prig as I did so. None of the staff or for that matter the scientists had the remotest idea what I was talking about. On the other hand Kitty spoke fluent French, Sir Jakub had a working knowledge, and Leila seemed to understand well enough. 'Excellent,' cried Kitty at the end. 'Most elegantly done, Ben. Anybody else?'

Sir Jakub volunteered. 'I will give you a little of my favourite poet,' he announced, his myopic eyes twinkling with bonhomie behind his bi-focal lenses. 'And perhaps Leila will translate.'

He then launched into *Kennst du das Land, wo die Zitronen blühn* from Goethe's *Wilhelm Meisters Lehrjahre*. He had a fine, resonant, actorish voice, and I was not surprised to hear later that he had in youth haunted the Vienna Burgtheater and even thought of renouncing science for the stage. Leila translated without hesitation. It occurred to me that she must know five languages pretty fluently: her mother's Russian, her father's

74

German, goodish French, schoolgirl Finnish, and the English in which she now thought and wrote.

So far it had all been somewhat up-the-market stuff. Bahadur now rose, majestic in his velvet smoking jacket, a large Havana in one hand, a glass of port in the other, and offered to contribute. 'I should like,' he said, 'to recite for you a few lines from that great poet whose genius may be said to derive as much from your country as from mine. I refer of course to the legendary Rudyard Kipling.' He then launched, to our intense surprise, into *The Ballad of East and West*, with somewhat comic effects:

Oh East is East, and West is West, and never the twain shall meet,
Till Earth and Sky stand presently at God's great Judgment Seat,
But there is neither East nor West, Border, nor Breed, nor Birth,
When two strong men stand face to face, though they come from the
    ends of the earth.

'Well done, Harry,' cried Kitty Haven, clapping hard. She always called him Harry, being unable to pronounce any of his real names.

'Come, Kitty,' said her husband coaxingly after a decent pause, 'give us some of your Russian songs.'

'Oh, very well then.' She was evidently only waiting to be asked, since Leila had the music ready on top of the piano. She preferred not to play the cello off duty, but she sang to us in a pleasing contralto, slow melancholy songs of her vanished motherland, and we couldn't help but be moved, despite not understanding a word. It seemed lèse-majesté to follow them, and there was a long pause.

'I'll sing for you,' said Roscoe suddenly. He rose, and launched with extraordinary verve into *Blaydon Races*. After that he sung a couple of good-humoured working-class songs:

Harry was a Bolshie, one of Lenin's lads,
Till he was finally slain by counter-revolutionary cads,

and then, even more drolly:

Oh I'm the man the very fat man that waters the workers' beer.

75

These simple and jolly songs were universally popular. For one thing we all knew what they meant. But after the song about the workers' beer he became more serious.

Without introduction, he launched into *La Bandiera Rossa*, with its rousing chorus:

Viva Communisma e la liberta!

'Ah yes,' said Sir Jakub at the end, nodding his head sadly. 'Indeed. If only we could have them both together.'

'We can,' said Daniel suddenly, unsmiling. 'We shall.'

Afterwards I asked Leila what she made of Daniel's contribution. She shrugged.

'Nothing much,' she said. 'He's your typical idealistic scientist; the brotherhood of man, the commonwealth of learning, from each according to his ability, to each according to his need; that sort of thing. When he has a Humber and a country house like Papa for winning the Nobel Prize he'll forget it all.'

'I suppose so,' I said.

23 I went up to Oxford in January 1948, and Leila came up to see me often, sometimes by car if she could scrounge her father's, more often by train. The young world was just recovering, not only from the worst war in history, but also the worst winter in memory. The city was full not only of blasé ex-colonels of twenty-five, still carefully wearing their officer's greatcoats and desert brothel-creepers, but also of precocious ex-schoolboys like Ken Tynan with his purple shirts, gold ties, dove-grey shoes, and famous stammer. Food and clothes were still rationed, nobody had much money, and yet there was such an access of pent-up spirits, such an embattled joie-de-vivre, such an uncorking of ungovernable ambitions, that the mass went critical and two or three dozen undergraduates there then became international names. There were some fabled moments: Leila and I were there the night an Oriel undergraduate called Sandy Wilson with some of his chums in the Experimental Theatre Club put on a review called *Ritzy, Regal and Super* which was a *succès fou;* the cheers seemed never to stop in that cheerless hall off the Woodstock Road and people were climbing in through the windows just to say they had been there. Among the little cast were Wilson himself and Tynan (it was the night he did that famous imitation of Robert Helpmann in which he suddenly stiffened like a ramrod, tip-toe, arms at attention, head swivelled in the eyes left position, with the immortal words: 'My God, there's an owl on my shoulder.'); a tubby, balding little South African called John Schlesinger sang some songs in that show and has since made a film or two. Tony Richardson was just coming up over the horizon with that theatrical Yorkshire lisp of his and we went to his sunburst production of *Troilus and Cressida*. The two most amazing *coups de théâtre*, however, were (a) Stanley Parker swaying on stage at the ETC revue in feathers, diamante, and

sequins, as Mae West. When I say as Mae West, I underpitch that quite extraordinary experience. What actually happened was that at the end of the show, and in the midst of the rapturous accolade, Tynan, one of the players, unbeknown to his fellow thespians, simply stepped forward, raised his hand, and told the dazzled audience, who by that time were ready to believe anything, that the fabled Mae West was with them direct from Beverly Hills. And then the lights swivelled, and there in drag stood Stanley Parker, Australian, courtier, courtesan, bit-player, party-thrower, farceur, sponger, poseur, boulevardier, gossip, wit, artist, part of my young days, floating in the limelight and loving his triumph. It was, I suppose, the greatest moment of his career.

Yes, and then (b) was Nevill Coghill's magical production of *The Tempest* by the lake of Worcester College in June 1949 when the players arrived by punt. At the end of the play each night Prospero threw an enormous volume into the water on that haunting line '*I'll drown my book*,' usually held to symbolise the end of Shakespeare's own life. It was an amazing inspiration of Coghill's to have Ariel run across the dark water of the lake on boards cunningly laid an inch below the surface. They played a floodlight on him as he raced back across the water again, round the bank away from the audience, up a concealed ramp to a high place above the trees where he threw up his arms as a flare exploded beneath him; and then every light in the garden went out so that the audience sat in stunned, momentary, velvet blackness. Leila was with me that night and the excitement of that visual triumph was transmuted, not for the first or last time in our lives, into a tremendous erotic charge; we strolled back to my little garret high up in Beaumont Street and, on the strength of it, made midsummer love. And the next morning with the early spring sun playing voyeur, we gave an encore, this time that sleepy congress that comes to lovers with the new dawn. Then we got up and went round to the covered market to eat fried egg sandwiches and drink strong, sweet tea with the stall holders; and after that we walked down to the river; and then we strolled back up the Cornmarket and drank coffee for an hour at Elliston and Cavell's; then I took Leila to a lecture on Stendhal I wanted to hear; and then it was time for some drinks in the Randolph. I've noticed since then that American universities are pretty well dry; certainly on the West Coast campuses you have to go two miles out to get your first drink. Oxford though, floated on a sea of alcohol; those days you could still get non-vintage champagne for around a pound a bottle. People drank beer with their friends and sherry with their tutors, and splashed on a bottle of wine if they wanted to try some grandiose seduction. It was not so much a liberal education as one gigantic, glorious, careless, non-stop party. Some people never recovered; some never really left.

It was still an essentially middle-class world. I can actually remember undergraduates who had their money in Consols; if it's still there it'll be worth roughly a sixth of what it was then and going down fast. In some senses, the university was still living in the 1930s; college servants still delivered coal to rooms in buckets and brought pitchers of hot water in the morning for you to shave in; there were men coming back who could clearly remember Richard Hillary when he was known only for rowing in the Trinity crew and *The Last Enemy* was a seed in his mind unfertilised by the sperm of death; there were dons in my own college who could remember the Provost telling the Bursar to go round at the beginning of the Michaelmas term and *make sure all the rooms were full*.

In 1948, of course, that worry had gone; the place bulged with the importunate and teeming young. I remember the little shuffling walk of Sir Edward Boyle embonpoint, an elder statesman of twenty-six, and the cool proto-Kennedy style of the embryo Wedgwood Benn, and honey-voiced Shirley Williams chaining herself to the railings of the Oxford Union to protest against the exclusion of women. I recall the famous lisp of Rees-Mogg, the bright panache of Jeremy Thorpe, the already ominous cross-examinations of the infant Robin Day. Tony Crosland was back from a good war with the Parachute Brigade, full of glamour and intelligence; and Kingsley Amis had not yet set off to teach English to Welshmen in Swansea with the consequences we all know. Maurice Bowra held his court in splendour at Wadham; his epigrams, as Cyril Connolly remarked, whistling over like unstoppable services; Trevor-Roper was writing his celebrated book on Hitler and A.J.P. Taylor his waspish history of inter-war England; David Cecil quacked and Isaiah Berlin boomed. Enid Starkie went to parties, as Bowra remarked, dressed in all the colours of the Rimbaud.

Leila and I went one night to Stanley Parker's rose party.

You had to wear a rose, and the only drink was vin rosé with rose petals floating in it, and only one tune, *La Vie En Rose*, was played all night. Most people were living like princes on an ex-service grant of £270 a year. And then all conditions of men came down to meet us; Attlee, the Prime Minister, spoke in his flat monologue on the cataclysmic changes over which he was quietly presiding; a great and grey man, as invincible as he was invisible.

I became secretary of a somewhat ludicrous dining club whose sole function was to hobnob with the literary establishment; I have still a postcard from Evelyn Waugh which I treasure and which reads: '*I cannot, or rather I will not, address your club.*' There is a note from Compton Mackenzie saying he will come with pleasure only we must promise him he need not wear a black tie nor sit down thirteen at table. I remember C. P. Snow delineating for us the critical path analysis of an imaginary young writer called — wasn't it? — H. V. Snodgrass. I remember the young Alan Brien interrupting a long but beautifully judged essay on Henry James by Tom Hopkinson, who was then incidentally editing *Picture Post*, with the brusque words: 'Look here, Mr. Hopkinson, this stuff about James is all very well, but how do we get on to your magazine?' And I remember Victor Gollancz calling for a jerry to have a piss in when his prostate began to trouble him in the midstream of his magnificently egocentric monologue.

I rowed every morning a little after dawn with seven other lunatics when the mist was still rising on the river and there was no sound but the splash of our oars. I rowed not so much for the exercise as for the chance to ease the mind; and in Eights Week Leila tied her stocking to our rudder, a fine old custom which I believe has now died, and we made four bumps. It was a time when the university could still seriously take on Australia at cricket and could field ten internationals against Cambridge at Twickenham; we were undefeated by them in my time there. *Et in Arcadia ego* — and yet, my diary, incorruptible chronicler, tells me that in the fifty-six days of the summer term, fried gold as a crisp in the deep fat of memory, I was in the depths of despair one day in three, just surviving most of the while, and happy only nine recorded times. What a mysterious experience is the function of mood; and what an unpredictable engine it is, driving us forward to our several fates.

24 The man who had digs directly beneath me in Beaumont Street was a very worthy and good man called Ronnie Townsend, who has finished up where life intended him, on the Tory back benches. There was really only one word for Ronnie then and now; the rather démodé adjective *sound*. Ronnie was certainly the soundest man I knew. He was a living tribute to the mysterious power of moderation in all things. He was rather square in build but by no means fat; he had a schoolboy's haircut and round, unfashionable glasses. His father was a Midlands businessman and he had sent Ronnie to Sedbergh where he'd done rather well. Ronnie was one of life's prefects. He was not, however, a prig. He worked steadily all week and each Saturday night would go out to Woodstock and drink four pints of draught bitter. He would then come back and — here was the bit for which I admired him — would remember to take his Alka-Seltzer before retiring to his virtuous couch, thus minimising the danger of repercussions the next morning. He had done well in the army out in Malaya, and had come back an acting half-colonel. He was college secretary of the university Conservative association, but otherwise did not essay to shine in university politics. He played squash three times a week for exercise. He got one of the most just degrees I ever heard of; a sound second based on eight papers to all of which the examiners had independently awarded exactly the same mark: beta plus. I suppose he was slightly boring, and yet the very even-ness of his character was somehow soothing. You always knew exactly where you stood with Ronnie. He took little or no interest in women until Leila brought Sue Carter up for Eights Week and, such is the mystical power of hormonal attraction, something in her honest peasant body, or was it her generous soul, turned Ronnie on alarmingly. His round glasses seemed positively to mist over with passion when I introduced them to each other. We took them to the Welsh Pony for a Scotch egg and a beer, and in the men's room to which we both shortly retired he could, most untypically, not restrain his excitement.

'I say, Ben,' he exclaimed, waving his well-mannered member at the wall, 'what a charming girl that is.'

'One of the best.'

'I wonder if I could ask her out to dinner.'

'I don't see why not. She's always hungry.'

'I take it that if I did it wouldn't queer your pitch.'

'Absolutely not. We're just good friends.'

'I wonder where I could take her. What sort of things does she like?'

'Steak and chips.'

'I do wish you could sometimes be serious, Ben.'

'So help me, Ronnie, steak and chips.'

'I see.' His honest face was troubled. 'I suppose the Randolph could provide a perfectly good steak and chips. What else does she like?'

'Rhubarb tart.'

'Ben, you're pulling my pisser.' By this time it was safely stowed, but it was still the rudest thing I'd ever heard Ronnie say.

'If you ask me, she's the one who's doing that.'

'I wish you wouldn't be so coarse, Ben.'

'Sorry, Ronnie.' He'd just lent me ten pounds, and was in every way a thoroughly decent man. 'Tell you what, I've just remembered. She loves game pie.'

'Aha.' Ronnie seemed relieved. 'I daresay the Mitre would do that all right.'

'Yes, but it's out of season.'

'Oh, sod it.'

'Who's being coarse now?'

'It's not funny, Ben.'

'Cold salmon. That's the ticket. And some cold Pouilly Blanc Fumé. Works a treat.'

'She enjoys wine?'

'She gargles with it.'

'I'll ask her tomorrow.'

'Good hunting, Ronnie.'

They were engaged by the end of the Trinity term, and married the following summer in the college chapel.

25 My love affair with Leila deepened all the time I was at university. Sometimes I used to catch a train to Paddington and we'd take one of those scruffy rooms in Sussex Gardens for the night; since then I've never driven down there without the authentic erotic frisson. Otherwise there were the vacations at Marston Mauditt, and the attic rooms in Paris and the rumpled beds in Florence, and in between she wrote me letters which I've never been able to throw away, though I've kept meaning to do so. I've always been suspicious of letters between lovers, suspecting them of being no more or less than exercises in self-indulgence; however, hers sometimes glinted with a sheen of simple passion which seemed worth preserving:

Ben my darling,
    Today I was in a conference with my father, ostensibly taking notes for him. But even as my pencil moved with demure dispatch over the pages of the notebook I was re-living last night and the sweet throb of you inside me and I wondered if any of those boring male faces round the table knew that the Professor's secretary was melting with remembered pleasure as they droned on and on and on. ...

Ben my darling,
    I suppose all happiness gets eroded away and all beauty dies and youth fades; dust hath closed Helen's eyes and so on; but there were moments the other night that were more important to me than anything else I've ever known or ever shall; and I shall always love you for those moments and never forget them as I may one day forget my address and my birth-place and the Lord's Prayer ... Life isn't conferences or shops or meals it's you and me young and aching and sobbing

83

with not two sorts of erotic experience, male and female, but one overwhelming flood of shared and indivisible delight . . .

Ben my darling,

Christ how I need you and long for you to be here again and to taste the particular and unforgettable pleasures of your young body . . . I ache for you and moan for you in my sleep and walk about all day in a daze and am sure the stupid people in the street can read the appalling hunger inside me which is never filled until you're there . . .

I went to Sotheby's the other day to buy some first editions in which I was interested and got fascinated by the letters and autographed manuscripts for sale the next day. Judging by some of the projected prices, I suppose Leila's letters must be worth several thousand now. And yet I'd be diminished without them in a totally unquantifiable way. What brutal work the auctioneer's hammer does to our encapsulated dreams and engrossed desires!

There was another side to Leila that few people knew. Just once as an undergraduate I was ill. Oxford is not the sort of place which caters for illness much and when my temperature, enraged by a nasty dose of some new virus, suddenly soared to 104, there was not much to be done except take to my bed and hope for the best. Ronnie came in several times with bottles of squash and packets of aspirin, which was civil of him; but when the temperature persisted he did something better; he rang Leila, who dropped everything and drove to Oxford at once. She sat by my bed for three days, feeding me bowls of soup, listening to my fevered ravings, changing my bed linen every time it grew damp with my sweat, and was still there holding my hand when I came through it safely on the fourth morning. I loved her for that.

On the other hand, there was the wretched business of the rhododendrons. On midsummer night, 1949, Ronnie and I threw a party. It was our turn, and we had a guest list of some fifty friends. We served champagne; but it's no use asking me how we could run to it. Admittedly you could get Veuve Cliquot for around thirty shillings in those days, but even that was some thirty shillings more than we could afford. I suppose the truth is that in that era you could run up credit, and in effect we paid for most of our pleasures after we had gone down. I know it took me two years to pay off all my debts.

That was the first time I'd ever met Charles Harbinger. Ronnie had been to one of his boring breakfasts, and been entranced by him. So there he was, tall, taut, and twitching, holding a glass of bubbly and talking earnestly about the pricing mechanism to a glazed group of gate-crashers, when Leila noticed him.

'Who's that?' she asked me.

'Who's what?'

'Who's that hungry, unhappy man in the grey flannel suit?'

'Oh him. His name's Harbinger. He's a friend of Ronnie's. A Rhodes Scholar from somewhere in New England. Why — want to meet him?'

'Not especially. Yes, all right.'

An hour later, the glazed group had melted away. Charles and Leila were in a corner and he was still talking but not, I fancied about the pricing mechanism. An hour after that, when I next got a glimpse through the haze, they had gone.

The party soared on its customary parabola, gathering speed till after midnight and then plummeting down to that quiet moment around three when the room still echoes with the last tune and the smoke still drifts in the air and the scent has only just begun to cloy. I was sitting in an armchair by that time, alone, staring vacantly into the middle distance, and not so much smashed as dazed, not so much outraged by Leila's disappearance as confused by it.

I was not quite alone though.

There was a girl sitting in the window seat on the other side of the room. Through the smoke I recognised her as somebody who had been brought along by one of Ronnie's athletic friends (Ronnie, I omitted to say, was not a bad runner; it was the only sport, he often used to tell me, in which no old boy network could prevail, the stopwatch being the ultimate and precise arbiter of excellence). This girl, though, did not look athletic; *au contraire*. She was smoking a cigarette with the greedy skill of a true addict; and she had in her hand a small tumbler of Scotch which must have come from our reserve bottle kept for those aristos of alcohol who touch nothing else.

'Hello,' she said.

I focussed rather uncertainly on her. She was an ash blond,

with good bones, a wide forehead, and what the French call *une bouche gourmande*.

'I'm sorry to be so rude. I must have been asleep.'

'You were a little preoccupied. Not really here.'

'It's just that someone I'm rather fond of has gone off with another man.'

'Yes, I saw. She'll be back.'

'How did you see? How do you know?'

'I saw by watching her. And him. And you. I know because I've done similar things myself.'

'I find that rather hard to believe.'

'It's because you find these things hard to believe that they happen to you.'

'You know an awful lot about me for someone who's never clapped eyes on me till this evening.'

'Not really. You see, I have occult powers.'

'You mean you're a witch?'

'Nothing so chic. But I do have second sight.'

'What does your second sight tell you now, for instance.'

'I can't tell from that distance. Come over here.'

I tottered rather unsteadily over and knelt beside her.

'Give me your hand.'

I handed it over. 'Ah.' She gave a low, melancholy sigh. 'Ah, yes. Now I see.'

'What do you see?' I had not meant to appear interested, but couldn't help myself.

'The two tragedies.'

'What two tragedies?'

'The two tragedies in your life.'

'Where are they, for God's sake?' I peered anxiously into my own palm. She held it in her hand with the cool interest of a fashionable 1930s doctor.

'You see those two crosses?'

'Where the creases meet?'

'Yes — those are the two tragedies.'

'By Christ, that's perceptive of you!'

'Why?'

'Because of course there *are* two tragedies in my life!' I was aflame with the excitement of my new self-knowledge.

'And what are they?'

'My parents of course. My father and mother!'

86

'Very good, Ben. You're an excellent subject. Responsive and sensitive.'

'How the devil did you know my name?'

'It was on the invitation card, dope. You don't need second sight for that.'

'No, of course not. How stupid of me.' I reflected. 'Still, you have to have some kind of inexplicable gift to know about the two tragedies.'

She grinned broadly at that. 'Yes, I do have amazing gifts.'

'What's your name?'

'Jill.'

'Yes, you look like a Jill.'

'And how, pray, do Jills look?'

'Like — uh, like a field of wheat. No sorry. They have minds like the wind on a sea of wheat.'

'Ah. You know your *Autumn Journal*.'

'Never heard of it. But I know my autumn wheat.'

'Liar. You've heard of it. The split vision of a juggler and the quick lock of a taxi . . . '

'And all of London littered with remembered kisses.'

'Time was away and somewhere else.'

'Two people with the one pulse.'

I took her hand. Her fingers curled gently round mine. The early morning sun stole in through the window like a fledgling housemaid and laid long fingers of buttered light before us. She smiled.

'*Le jour se lève.*'

'I've always wanted some charming woman to say that to me at this hour, but I thought she'd be French.'

'Sorry. I'm from Wiltshire.'

'That was obvious.'

'I'm the one with occult powers, remember?'

'At least, it was obvious once you'd said it.'

'I must go.'

'Not yet.'

'There'll be another time.'

'You can be so sure?'

'I'm sure.'

'And how shall I find you?'

'My other name's Maysey. You can get me at St. Anne's, or

out of term time at Shallerton in Wiltshire. We've been farming there for three hundred years.'

'I'm from next door. Hampshire. We've been farming other people's land there since the middle ages.'

She laughed.

'Anyway, we're both from Hardy country.'

'Yes, of course, we've got that in common too. Which one's your favourite?'

'*The Woodlanders.*'

'Agreed. *You was a good man, and did good things.*'

'One of the ten best lines in the language.'

'And the others?'

'I'll tell you next time. Goodbye.'

She kissed me in a way that was neither perfunctory nor predatory, but thoughtful, as if she wanted to imprint the memory on her mind. And then I felt a very light shiver run through her; the kind that only happens at that hour of morning when every nerve is tautened and each sensation laser-sharp. Time was away and somewhere else.

Then it was over, and she looked at me a long moment before picking up her things.

'Thank you for having me.'

'Thank you for coming.'

I was still asleep in the ruins of the party when Leila kissed me awake at noon. She was still in her party dress. She looked, for her, rueful.

'Somebody else kissed you to sleep and it's all my fault.'

'Contrition doesn't become you.'

'And you're not even angry.'

'Just curious.'

'Charles wanted to show me these rhododendrons. He said he'd never seen anything so beautiful. They're in the grounds of an enormous house in Kent which belongs to a friend of his father. So we just got in his car and went to see them.'

'Were they worth the trip?'

'Yes.'

'And what have you done with him?'

'Charles? Oh, he drove me back. We stopped at The Rose Revived for breakfast and then he had to go to a seminar.'

'Oh my God.'

'He's dreadfully unhappy, Ben.'

'So was I.' But it didn't ring true.

She looked at me carefully for a long minute.

'I made a very bad mistake last night,' she said. 'I didn't realise how bad until just now.'

'How do you mean?'

'I don't know exactly what I mean. But I know it all right.'

'You're talking rubbish. Let's forget it ever happened.'

But I never forgot that night and nor did she.

26 Next Easter I was busy doing what revision I could before Schools in June and Leila was away again with her father at a conference in Geneva. Strolling one evening round the lake to get a breather from my books, I came across Daniel sitting morosely by the bank. I sat down beside him.

'Hello, Daniel. May I join you?'

He hardly looked up. 'Hello, Ben. Yes. Yes, of course.'

'You look rather low, Daniel.'

'Do I? Sorry.' He pulled a blade of grass and sucked it. 'But there's a lot to be depressed about, isn't there?'

'For instance.'

'I'm worried about my father.'

'What's wrong with him?'

'He's out of work.'

'In this day and age?'

'Sure. You don't know what it's like up north, Ben. Up in the north-east anyway.'

'I thought there was tons of work.'

'There was. Ever since the war they were busy. A bloody fine reason for full employment but as you know, the most effective one. And since the war they've been catching up with all the backlog of work they should have done in the war. And now there's no work again.'

'At least we've got a socialist government.'

'A what? You don't call this load of milksops a socialist government, do you?'

'They've pushed through a lot of legislation — the National Health Service, nationalised steel and railways, given India independence.'

'And arse-crawled to the Yanks on every major foreign policy issue.'

'They haven't had much choice.'

'Of course they have a choice. They could have chosen real socialism.'

'Ah.' I had never delved too deeply into Daniel's politics, nor anyone else's at Marston Mauditt for that matter. I somehow assumed that all the Haven family were solid middle-of-the-road social democrats who would vote for Attlee's government as a matter of course.

Daniel stared into the water gloomily, the very portrait of a chronic dyspeptic. I knew he had had a duodenal ulcer and that in my book explained a lot. 'It's so corrupt, Ben,' he said at length. 'The whole bloody system.'

'But at least we have a choice. That's the only thing they can never lay claim to on the other side; the luxury of doubt.'

'Ha!' He spat out his chewed-up cud of grass. 'Listen, young bloody bourgeois Ben, what choice do you think my father had before the war when two hundred of them had to go down to the shipyard gate and stand there while the gaffer picked out one man in three?'

'What's the good of looking back? It's a new world.'

'Do you know how much my father makes when he is working? Six pounds. Seven pounds when things are good.'

'Is he bitter?'

'You mean is he bitter like me?' Daniel gave one of his wry grins. 'No, he's not bitter. He thinks Attlee and his shower are the cat's whiskers. He's got his books and his music.'

'I didn't realise — '

'You didn't realise that the working class could read and write — is that it, Ben?'

'No of course not.'

'My father has the complete works of Shakespeare on his shelves,' Daniel said almost to himself. 'He bought on the never-never from Odhams. And the works of Dickens. Same source. And he's got the works of Robbie Burns by his bed, like a good Geordie. And the Bible. That's the bloody trouble. He still goes in for that pap.'

'Tell me what music he likes.'

Daniel looked at me quickly to make sure my question was a serious one, then said offhandedly, 'Nothing very complex. Tchaikovsky's First Symphony. Mendelssohn's Italian Sym-

phony. But that's the way in, isn't it, Ben? That's the way to
Opus 135.'

'He must be very proud of you.'

Daniel laughed, but there was no humour in his laughter.

'Oh sure. The bright boy of the family. The scholarship lad.
The swot who got on and won an open scholarship to Cambridge. And did all right in the Tripos. And worked in the
Cavendish with all the brightest boffins in the land. And used
his intelligence to help in the biggest murder of all time.'

'We had no choice.'

'What was wrong with the open sea?'

'I don't think it had quite sunk in what they were going to do
with that thing.'

'Hadn't it? Well, I was at Los Alamos and I saw it and I
knew. And so did a lot of other people who should have known
better.'

'I don't see what a scientist can do. What if they'd got there
first?'

'They were nowhere near. Miles away. If he'd kept that team
they had at Vienna in 1936, it would have been a different story.
But of course they were all Jews. Ironic really, but right that
they should have delivered the final come-uppance. It's corrupt,
Ben. It's prostitution.'

'Does the Professor think the same way as you?'

'I think in his heart he does. But he's too old and full of
honours, too sold out to care any more.'

'But you're not.'

'I still care.'

He stared moodily into the lake.

'Have you heard of heavy water, Ben?'

'Yes.'

'Have you ever seen it?'

'No.'

'I have.'

'What's it like?'

'Common or garden household water. But it's not at all
ordinary. It's quite extraordinary in fact.' He seemed genuinely
excited now; exalted almost.

'Where did you see it?'

'At Cambridge. Two French scientists called Halban and
Kowarski brought the entire world stock over here in 1940. The

92

French bought it from a Norwegian firm and got it to Scotland by plane, then on an express train to London in thirteen cans — about a hundred and eighty-five kilogrammes of it.'

'And from there to Cambridge?'

'No — to France. It was hidden in all sorts of odd places as the Germans advanced — a woman's prison for instance — and finally a strange English peer called Lord Suffolk commandeered a boat at Bordeaux and brought the water and all the industrial diamonds and about fifty scientists home from France to Britain again.'

'Why is it so important?'

'Because it's a mixture of oxygen and the heavy isotope of hydrogen. This heavy bit reduces the speed of neutrons but doesn't absorb them. You have to have slow neutrons to cause the uranium nucleus to split. Heavy water, in fact, is what we call a moderator, and pretty nearly ideal it is too.'

'Did Fuchs know about heavy water?'

The trial of Klaus Fuchs for betraying atomic secrets had only recently been completed.

'Good God, yes. And a damn sight more.'

'Did you know him?'

'Klaus? Yes. I worked with him in America.'

'What was he like?'

'Dedicated. Humourless. Arrogant.'

It occurred to me that this was how most people saw Daniel himself; though I saw more in him than that.

'Why did he do it?'

Daniel turned and looked straight at me. I'd never noticed before that his eyes were an unsettling and aqueous pale green.

'Because he had the power.'

'How do you mean?'

'In human life, how many men ever have the power to affect their own lives?'

'Precious few.'

'Right. And how many would you say, held in the hollow of their hands the power to change the balance of world power?'

'Maybe half-a-dozen.'

'Klaus had that power. And he used it. Not for narrow ideological reasons, you see. Simply because he thought he knew best.'

'What appalling arrogance.'

Daniel looked at me again, his fingers trailing the reedy water of Marston Mauditt lake. Water was his element; it fascinated him. Then he said, but more, I thought, to himself, 'Yes, it was bloody arrogant. But in a way, magnificent. After Klaus went over, nothing in the world was ever the same again. He did more damage than all the spies in history of all nationalities in all the wars put together. Imagine, Ben.'

'Christ, how awful.'

'Only if he was wrong, Ben. But if he was right, how wonderful.'

27 One day soon after that I got a note from Oliver Debenham:

Dear Ben,
    I'm bringing the Professor to Oxford on Tuesday for a conference. Any chance we might have a jar together? It'd be nice to have a natter.
                          All the best,
                          Oliver.

I suggested we should meet in a pub called the Turf. It had a conspiratorial flavour which I felt would appeal to Oliver's intricate spirit. When I got there, slightly out of breath from the Taylorian, he was already ensconced in a corner with a pint of bitter. I bought one too, and sat beside him with some ill-formed sense of anticipation. He was always good value, and I felt isolated from Marston Mauditt, however many letters I got from home. Oliver looked well. He had at last married Milly, and she was expecting their first child. He had always been an attractive male animal, and the first streaks of silver in his glossy black hair seemed to help. His face was ruddy and free of care, and he was always well turned out in dark blue suits. When he occasionally accompanied Sir Jakub on foreign trips, he was usually mistaken for a colleague. He had raised a talent for gossip into an art form.
    'Well, Ben,' he began, 'how's life?'
    'Not bad, Oliver. I've got finals this summer, so shades of the prison house begin to close. But apart from that, no problems.'
    'Good.' He drank beer, and seemed oddly reticent. I decided to prompt him.
    'How are things at home?'
    'Oh fine. Your grandparents are both well.'

'And Leila?'

'Lovely as ever.' He peered into his glass. 'A bit too lovely, maybe.'

'How do you mean?'

Oliver looked up at me quickly, then down into the fascinating depths of his beer again.

'Well, she sees a good deal of this fellow Roscoe.'

'That's hardly surprising. They work together.'

'Bit more than work, I reckon.'

'For instance?'

He looked as crestfallen as if he had muffed a gear change.

'I don't know, Ben, and it's really none of my business, but they're always out together. She's always driving him in the Professor's car when he's away — '

'Ah, that's what you don't like.'

'No, it's not that, Ben. In fact, she's a handy driver. Good as a man you might say. And clean and tidy with it. Always brings her back as if she hasn't been out of the garage. No — '

'I was only joking.'

'I know you were, Ben. No — they're always walking round that blasted lake, talking and talking.'

'Sounds harmless enough to me.'

'But it's the *way* they talk. The *way* they look at each other. Milly mentioned it first. You know how women notice these things.'

'You intrigue me.'

He did. It was a conjunction I hadn't imagined. It struck me as improbable. But then, as I'd already begun to see, nothing that concerns men and women is all that improbable. What curious taste she evinced; Toby, a crypto-fascist bully-boy, Daniel (if it were true about Daniel) an introverted, screwed-up loner, and myself, a romantic, untutored loon. There was only one attribute we had in common. We were all men. No, there was another. We were all there. Perhaps Leila had not so much taste as appetite. Who could tell?

28 One iridescent morning in May I came out of the Taylorian around twelve-thirty and crossed St. Giles to the Lamb and Flag; a thing I did every day in life. It was near and it was cheap and it was quick and the beer was good. I ordered a pint of bitter and a sandwich, my normal lunch, sat down in a corner and settled into the book I had with me. On the bricks of many such ordinary moments are our lives built; but at that quite unremarkable instant my life was about to change for ever. I sensed that someone was looking at me, and I didn't like the sensation. I glanced up, and realised that I was being closely watched by a small, sharp, neat man who wore rimless glasses, a dark blue blazer, gaberdine trousers, a white shirt with button-down collar, and a sober blue tie. Seeing that I had caught his eye, he came over and addressed me in one of those stateless accents that make the hair on the back of your neck crawl.

'Mr. Freeman?'

'Yes.'

'May I introduce myself?' He took out a thin wallet and produced a card, which he handed me. It said:

PHILIP RUNE

and then, in the bottom lefthand corner: *Investigatory Reporter.*

'How do you do, Mr. Rune,' I said.

'I must apologise for staring at you like that.'

'I was mystified, mainly.'

'You're not used to people taking a special interest in you?'

'Absolutely not.'

'I'm sorry. It's a fine thing, privacy.'

'Yes.'

'Can I get you a drink?'

'No thanks. I have to work this afternoon.'

'Of course. I'm sorry. Then let me explain.' He sat down

beside me, a taut, dapper little man with an inquisitive nose. Indeed his nose, I reflected later, was much his best feature. It had character, if not charm.

'I'll not beat about the bush, Mr. Freeman,' he said. 'I'm interested in a scientist called Daniel Roscoe and I believe you know him.'

'Yes. Why the interest?'

'He went to Finland recently.'

'That's right. He needed a holiday. He was overdoing it. Professor Haven lent him their place to wind down a bit.'

'You obviously know Leila Haven too?'

'Yes. Why?'

'Did you know she flew out to Finland a couple of days after Roscoe?'

'No. But I'm not all that surprised. She was trying to help him.'

'Did you know that they both crossed the border into Russia yesterday?'

'No. But so what?'

'They had no visas for Russia when they left London. Nor did they cross at any of the established places. They were — taken across.'

'You mean against their will?'

'I don't think so.'

'Why are you telling me all this?'

'I thought she might have left you a note. I believe she was a good friend of yours.'

'She still is.'

'Really, Mr. Freeman? Hasn't she — ah — let you down rather?'

'Not in any sense that you'd understand. Anyway, what business is it of yours?'

'I've already explained, Mr. Freeman. It's my job.'

'Who do you do your investigating for exactly?'

'Various people. Whoever retains me.'

'And who's retained you this time?'

'That, I'm afraid, I'm not at liberty to say.'

'Then why should I feel at liberty to answer your questions?'

'I might be able to help you.'

'I don't need any help.'

'But you might when the — er — authorities arrive.'

98

'What authorities?'

'Well, I should have thought the security people are bound to be interested.'

'Why?' I knew perfectly well why, but wanted to hear him spell it out.

'Oh come, Mr. Freeman. Let's not be naive. Roscoe had access to an awful lot of classified information. He could be extremely useful on the other side.'

'We've no proof yet that he's gone willingly, that if he has gone willingly he's going to stay, or that if he's going to stay he's going to disclose classified information.'

'No, Mr. Freeman, we've no proof. But we have to face the unhappy probabilities, don't we now?'

'I'll wait till the security people come — if indeed they ever do.'

'I'm very close to them, Mr. Freeman. You can take it from me they'll be here.'

'We'll see. Anyway, I can't accept that Leila has done anything to get across them.'

'She could have talked him into going.'

'Not a chance.'

'I wonder why you're so positive?'

'She took no political stance. She was an intensely . . . private person.'

'People defect for all sorts of reasons, Mr. Freeman. Sometimes of course it is simply an ideological motivation. Sometimes it is cupidity. Sometimes there is an emotional or even psychotic cause. Sometimes you have the interesting position where it is not a defection at all, merely a realignment with one's original side.'

'That could hardly apply to Roscoe.'

'No, but it could to the Haven family.'

'Rubbish.'

'Ah. How nice it must be, Mr. Freeman, to be so young and so certain.'

'You are the one who seems to know what is certain.'

'Probable, Mr. Freeman. Only probable. But why don't you tell me a little about Daniel and Leila? After all, we're on the same side, aren't we?'

'I don't know what side you're on. But I do know I'm on nobody's side.'

'Isn't that a trifle indiscreet of you in this day and age, Mr. Freeman?'

'If it is, I'm in good company.'

'Really? I wonder if the authorities would agree with that?'

'We shall have to see, shan't we? Now if you'll excuse me, I have to go back to work.'

'Very well, Mr. Freeman. I daresay we shall meet again. You are a very loyal young man, personally loyal, but you must remember there is more than one kind of loyalty.'

'I'd like you to remember that, too, Mr. Rune.' I felt a quick wave of a powerful, complex emotion; anger certainly, but also an unidentified fear, and the beginning of a lifelong antipathy for Mr. Rune and all his race. He bowed very slightly, showing the neat white parting in his glossy hair.

'*A bientôt*, Mr. Freeman.'

'*Fous-moi la paix*, Mr. Rune.'

29 There was, as it turned out, a letter waiting for me from Leila when I got back to my room in Beaumont Street:

Ben Darling,
   I have to go away for a while. Don't be hurt, don't be shocked, don't be surprised. Just accept that there are good reasons. I can't explain yet. Only trust me. Never doubt my love — L.

That was all. I sat on my bed pondering it for a while. Then I picked up the telegram that had been waiting too. I knew what it was going to say:
Please come home at once. Important. It was signed simply, *Haven.* I threw a few things into a bag and caught the next train home.

As we drove up the hill to Marston Mauditt, I could already sense the change in the place. It had lost its innocence. The Pitcher of Good Ale was under siege for the first time since the Civil War. There were half-a-dozen sleek cars parked outside and a BBC television van. There were more cars parked outside and all the way up the drive of the Havens' house, and there was a graceful Lagonda on the cobbles outside my grandparents' cottage.

I found them in the front parlour perched nervously on the edge of their chairs. With them were two strangers, a bloated man of fifty and a harridan of somewhere the same age with untidy peroxide hair and nails bitten down to the quick. The man got up as I came in.

'Ah, this must be young Mr. Freeman. How do you do. My name is Barton King and this is my colleague Helen Reddish.'

I was not too well up in the Fleet Street hall of fame, but even

I had heard of these two, and I filled in the details later. Barton King was a bank clerk's son who had won scholarships to Oxford where he had got a first in Mods and a fourth in Greats. After his first disastrous marriage he had drifted from teaching into court reporting, where his graceful pen had attracted the attention of two vying press lords. After a hectic auction, he had been launched on his career as a columnist and peripatetic correspondent, and was said to be the highest-paid man in the business.

The Lagonda was one of the rewards of his calling; as indeed was the gross over-indulgence which had comprehensively botched his once promising face. Helen Reddish had been born in a Rochdale back-to-back which may have excused her subsequent career if indeed anything could.

'Mr. Freeman,' King began winningly. 'We'd be so grateful for your help. My paper has sent us down here to cover this dreadful business and your grandparents have been enormously kind to us. But it is of course you who knew Daniel best — '

'And Leila,' put in Helen Reddish. They were already on first name terms with two human beings they had never met.

'What can I tell you?' I sat down and poured myself a glass of my grandfather's dandelion wine. It was already three-quarters gone.

'Did Daniel ever talk to you about his political beliefs?'

'Hardly. He was a dedicated scientist — not a political animal at all.'

'But of course, as we've alas seen, the pure scientist is often the most naive politically,' King put in quickly. 'The kind of personality most likely to be swayed by coarse-grained political argument?'

'I think Daniel knew exactly where he stood.'

'Did he ever talk about — ah, the other side — about Russia?'

'Never.'

'Did he ever criticise the Western position in the international power game?'

'I can't imagine him ever talking in those terms.'

'Was he a bitter man?' It was her question.

'That would be too dramatic. He was sometimes — a shade disappointed.'

'With what? With his country? His job?'

'I think you ought to talk to his colleagues about this. Or his family.'

'We shall of course be doing that. But naturally, we must get as rounded a portrait as possible.'

'He was a hard-working, conscientious sort of chap,' said my grandfather. 'If he had a piece of work on he'd worry away about it all night until he'd solved it. I've often found him still awake in the lab when I've started work at six.'

'How interesting,' King interposed politely.

'I don't think he was that healthy,' said my grandmother. 'Many's the time I've seen him leave half his dinner uneaten.'

'Fascinating,' murmured Helen Reddish.

'Tell us about Leila, Mr. Freeman,' King appealed to me. 'I believe she was a particularly good friend of yours.'

'She still is.'

'Yes, of course. She must be quite a remarkable young lady.'

'She wasn't a lady.'

'But a real woman.' That was Helen Reddish again.

'I don't know what an unreal woman would be like.'

'Frightfully good, Ben,' cried King, swigging his dandelion wine to the dregs and settling it hopefully on the table for more. 'I like that.'

'Was she in love with Roscoe?' Helen Reddish again.

'Good God, no.'

'Was she in love with you?'

'She despised language like that.'

'That doesn't answer my question.'

'Frankly I don't see why I should answer it.'

'I think you have, Ben,' King put in amiably. 'What delicious wine that is, Mrs. Freeman.'

'I'll find another bottle,' she said, and bustled out.

'Were you lovers?' That was Helen Reddish.

I got up. 'I'm extremely sorry but I must go and see Professor Haven. He is naturally extremely upset.'

'Yes, we know. We've seen him already.'

There were about a dozen men trespassing on the Havens' back lawn but I managed to get through them and into the kitchen which was being guarded by the Debenhams. Oliver bolted the door after me. He was chalk-white with anger.

'Do you know what the bastards did?'

'No — what?'

'Offered us a hundred quid for our story.'

'What did you do?'

'Told them to stuff it, of course. I've had a bit to do with this sort when I was with my previous employer, the Hon. Reginald Farthing. Dirty muck-rakers. Mind you — ' and he sat down again at the kitchen table and stirred his tea thoughtfully — 'Reggie did have a skeleton or two in the cupboard. And God knows how many bits of fluff. I suppose I could sell my memoirs one day.'

'You'll do nothing of the kind, Oliver Debenham,' said Milly with sudden force. 'Not after Sir Jakub and Lady Kitty have been so kind to us.'

'I was only joking, love,' said Oliver soothingly. 'None of these bastards will get a thing out of me except a swift kick in the crotch. I've rung the police already. But there's two gents from the Yard, some top brass, with the Professor right now. Say they want to see us all.'

'Christ, not again.'

'Well, these chaps are here on official business, Ben. They're looking after the nation's security, after all.'

'O.K., I'll wait. Give us some tea, Milly dear.'

It was a full hour before the internal telephone rang. Oliver answered. He grimaced over the mouthpiece.

'You're on, Ben.'

I went through the dining room and drawing room into Professor Haven's study. He was looking grey, and the stubble on his unshaven face did not help. With him were the two gents Oliver had mentioned.

'Ben, my dear boy,' Haven began. 'Thank you so much for coming. These two gentlemen are trying to help us with this dreadful case.'

'This,' and he indicated a lean, under-fed man of about forty with a face like the inside of an old but much-loved tobacco pouch, 'is Commander Sparkenbrooke from the Special Branch.'

'How do you do, Commander.'

'And this is Mr. John Chaffinch from the Foreign Office.'

Chaffinch was about the same age but half a head shorter. He had a sweet smile and thinning blond hair brushed hopefully over the dome of his head. He looked queer to me; but then so did a lot of Englishmen of his age and class.

'How do you do, Mr. Chaffinch.'

'Mr. Freeman, we think you might be able to help us,' Sparkenbrooke began.

'I'll do my best.'

'First of all, tell us everything you can about yourself. I'll take you through the main headings one by one.'

'Go ahead.'

It took about half an hour and was quite an impressive performance. I noticed a tape recorder turning lazily on the table. When I'd done with the somewhat pedestrian story of my life, Chaffinch took over.

'Mr. Freeman, you were close to Roscoe?'

'Not all that close. I liked him, and we'd talk by the lake sometimes. But he was a solitary, introspective sort of person.'

'You no doubt discussed politics?'

'Not in the sense you might mean. But he did express dissatisfaction with the Attlee government. He said what we wanted was real socialism.'

'And did he specify what he meant by real socialism?'

'He didn't have to do that.'

'How do you mean?'

'Daniel came from the north-east. His family were all shipbuilders and miners. They were unemployed throughout the thirties, and now they're unemployed again. Many of his family are communists. I imagine he was one too.'

The two security men exchanged glances.

'There was nothing in his security clearance about belonging to the party,' said Sparkenbrooke.

'He made no secret of it,' Haven broke in. 'He sang *Bandiera Rossa* for us one Christmas.'

'Many of us have done that in our time without being actually *communists*,' Chaffinch reproved him in his pansy voice.

'Of course. But let's not beat about the bush. If I'd ever been asked about this before the present unhappy business, I'd have said unhesitatingly that he was a communist. But that doesn't of course have the dire connotations it does in America. The assumption here is that a man may sincerely be a communist and a patriot too.'

'Not when he's an undeclared communist working on classified information,' Sparkenbrooke put in.

'Frankly,' said Haven, 'I never gave it a thought. Daniel was a brilliant scientist. Possibly the best pure physicist under thirty-five in the country. My interest in him was purely professional.'

'Of course, Professor,' Sparkenbrooke soothed him gently. 'But naturally we have to look at it differently.'

'And did he ever talk about Los Alamos?' Chaffinch suddenly cut in.

'Yes, once. He said he'd got conned into taking part in a murder or words to that effect.'

'Ah. An idealist dissident.' Chaffinch seemed pleased with his deduction.

'There was no question — he thought our system totally corrupt,' I added.

'That would add up,' said Sparkenbrooke.

'Indeed,' Chaffinch summed up, 'there is no mystery whatsoever about Mr. Roscoe's disappearance — for that is all it so far is — except our failure to notice his predicament and — ah — float him in slightly less troubled waters.'

'We shall have our own post-mortem later,' Sparkenbrooke cut in grimly. 'Now Mr. Freeman, if we may, what about Miss Haven?'

'I'm as baffled as you are.'

'She was,' and here Chaffinch smiled winningly 'your girlfriend, I suppose?'

'Yes. We were close.'

'And did she ever discuss politics with you?' Sparkenbrooke wanted to know.

'Frankly no. She struck me as a totally a-political person. But — '

'Yes?' Chaffinch prodded me gently.

'She was a loner. A maverick. She went her own way. She would never have been beholden to any human being, man or woman; she was one of the most independent people I've ever met.'

'And her relationship with Roscoe,' Sparkenbrooke asked. 'Was he a rival of yours?'

'I find it hard to believe. Oliver — he's Oliver Debenham, the chauffeur here, told me they had long talks together in my absence. But if you mean were they lovers — '

'We had an interesting talk to his mother and father and married sister this morning,' Chaffinch volunteered. 'They told us he had shown no interest in girls at all in his youth. He was far too interested in excelling at his scientific work. However, there was one girl of whom he was fond.'

He had my full attention now.

'Her name is Brenda McCarthy. Or at least was until she became Brenda Sullivan on her marriage. She too was a gifted, hard-working child from an unprivileged background. They went to school and university together.'

'He never mentioned her,' I broke in.

'Possibly not. One of our people had a long talk with Mrs. Sullivan this morning. She reluctantly volunteered the information that he was impotent.'

'Poor old sod,' I said involuntarily.

'As you so graphically put it, Mr. Freeman,' said Chaffinch, 'poor old sod. Now there is, of course, a certain kind of woman who may find impotence a challenge. Would Miss Haven come into that category?'

I thought it over.

'Everything's possible,' I said at length. 'But in Leila's case — oh, I forgot. She left me a note. Here it is.'

'Ah.' They put their heads together over it.

'And you were left nothing, Sir Jakub?' Sparkenbrooke asked.

'Nothing. That is why my wife is so heartbroken.'

'What are we to make of Miss Haven's case,' Chaffinch asked the ceiling. 'An undercover party member? A secret mistress of Roscoe? An idealist dedicated to restoring some imagined balance of terror? Or do we have to assume that she was simply her father's daughter?'

'What the devil do you mean by that?' Haven asked very quietly.

'Sir Jakub, I have to ask all the questions my masters are going to ask me, and then I have to think out the answers. In your case I have no doubt at all about the answer. But I have to have it ready.'

'I'm sorry,' Haven said.

Chaffinch thoughtfully changed the tape.

'Tell us if you will, Mr. Freeman,' he said with some charm, 'everything you can remember about Miss Haven. I'll take you through the ground section by section. Will you try to help us?'

'Yes, of course. Go ahead.'

30 When I got back to Oxford I was still suffering from delayed shock. Schools were four weeks away, but I seemed unable to focus on the fact. I sat in my room that first evening staring into space. Ronnie found me there.

'Now then, Ben,' he admonished me. 'This won't do. We can't have you sitting there moping. You're coming to the theatre with me tomorrow evening. I've made up a party and we'll go to the Taj for supper afterwards. It'll do you good.'

'Thanks, Ronnie, but I'd rather not. Frankly I'm still feeling distinctly odd.'

'Stuff and balderdash.' Ronnie could be firm when he wished. 'I simply will not take no for an answer. I've asked Jill Maysey to keep you company.'

'Oh. Well thanks, Ronnie. It's very kind of you. I hardly know her.'

'That doesn't matter. I don't know her either, but I've always thought she looked the sort of girl one would be able to tell one's troubles to.'

The play was not up to much, and Ronnie's friends not very inspiring, though I knew they were trying desperately hard not to be tactless. At one point during supper afterwards, Ronnie launched into a long harangue about *The God That Failed* which he'd been reading. He'd just got to the bit in Koestler's essay about the enormous gap in pay between a Russian general and private when he looked across at me and remembered and abruptly changed the subject.

'It was as if,' I said later to Jill when we'd got back to my place in Beaumont Street, 'I'd suffered a bereavement.'

'In a sense you have,' she replied. She sat by the fire smoking and drinking her customary small tumbler of whisky.

'You haven't asked me anything about it.'

108

'I knew you'd tell me what you wanted to tell me when you were ready.'

'I haven't talked to anyone about it except the security people.'

'And the press.'

I laughed ruefully at that. In my drawer there were a pile of cuttings. They were more or less accurate as far as they went; but accuracy is not truth. The prize exhibit for me, however, was a page from the paper which employed Barton King and Helen Reddish on such munificent terms. King had kicked off first:

Stark tragedy stalked the beautiful stones of Marston Mauditt yesterday.

Here the great atomic scientist Sir Jakub Haven has made his home. Here he has unravelled some of the most vital secrets of atomic energy.

In doing so he has repaid the country that gave him a refuge from the Nazis.

It is a debt he finds difficult to express in words.

He said to me yesterday on the billiard-table lawn of Marston Mauditt: 'It is impossible for me to explain what my work has contributed to atomic physics.'

His most brilliant pupil Daniel Roscoe, 35, who defected to Russia, carrying with him all the Professor's precious secrets, had no doubts about his role.

'He was a dedicated scientist,' a family friend, 24 year old Mr. Ben Freeman told me yesterday.

But isn't a pure scientist just the kind of man most likely to be swayed by naive political argument?

'Daniel knew exactly where he stood,' Mr. Freeman confirmed.

'He was a disappointed man,' he added.

And a desperately worried one.

'He would worry all night,' said Mr. William Freeman, Ben's grandfather and bailiff at the Marston Mauditt farm. 'I've often found him still awake in the lab at six in the morning.'

And his health was cracking under the strain.

'Many's the time I've seen him leave half his dinner uneaten,' Rosanna Freeman, William's wife, explained.

Back home on Tyneside his Geordie father, 62 year old ship-worker Arthur Roscoe, was too upset to talk of the tragedy. But a neighbour said: 'He was a studious lad. Not standoffish but shy. His dad was very proud of him. Now the whole street knows it has a traitor in its midst.'

Helen Reddish had written a separate article about Leila:

Key enigma in the great drama unfolding at Marston Mauditt is the mysterious half-Russian girl Leila Haven.
Leila is the daughter of Sir Jakub and his wife Kitty, the famous musician.
She was young, beautiful, tempestuous — and she already had a stormy past.
She left Cambridge, where she was a medical student, after a row with the authorities which has still not been explained.
Yesterday her college refused to comment on the case.
But Sarah Jascot, now a London G.P., remembers her well.
She told me yesterday: 'The whole thing was just a storm in a teacup. It was one of those emotional storms that sometimes blow up in a women's college involving another girl and a jealous female don.
'The whole thing was a joke really. Leila left in disgust at their narrow-mindedness. She wasn't sent down.
'She was certainly the most unusual person I knew there.'
Since then, blond, green-eyed Leila has become the centre of a tangled love triangle at Marston Mauditt.
Two men fell in love with her.
One was Daniel Roscoe, the brilliant working-class scientist. The other was Ben Freeman, shy 24 year old Oxford student. Yesterday Ben was too upset to say much.
'She was a real woman,' he told me.
Now she is in Russia with Roscoe.
Once again, a woman has chosen the tug of love above the call of duty.

Jill read both stories with great care and without smiling.
'She makes you sound rather nice.'
'She makes me sound a complete twerp.'
'Why don't you get it out of your system. Tell me what really happened.'

'It would take a long time.'

'Tell me.'

Ronnie was right: she was a good person to tell one's troubles to. When at last I'd come to the end of the melancholy chronicle, I said: 'But I've done all the talking. And I still know nothing about you.'

'There's not much to tell.'

'Go on.'

So she told me about her father, who was a charmer but weak and lazy, her mother who had tried to marry her off to a local nob called Nigel, her brother Peter who was ambitious and tough; about their farm and their house at Shallerton which was 300 years old; and about her love affair with a dreadful Frenchman called Gaston. Then she told me that she was going to write children's books one day. We found that apart from Hardy, we both liked Auden, MacNeice, and Spender. She was appalled to hear that I hadn't yet read *Middlemarch* and promised to lend it to me. Then it came out that the only Herrick I knew were the three poems in the *Oxford Book of English Verse*, so she promised to lend me the collected works. I was just recovering from *Brideshead Revisited* which I'd found magical; she preferred the pre-war novels, especially *Vile Bodies*. We were both hooked on *The Unquiet Grave*. She had read much more in the English language than I had, but she had odd gaps. I lent her my copy of the letters of Madame de Sévigné which she'd never read. She didn't share my veneration for Hemingway; his heroines were such ghastly goodies. We both thought most of Scott Fitzgerald unreadable.

At length we fell silent until she suddenly said:

'There's a bit of Chaucer I particularly like. It goes:

> *"Clean out of your mind*
> *Ye have me cast, and I can ne may*
> *for all this worlde within my herte find*
> *to unloven you a quarter of a day"* '

There was another long silence.

'It's dawn again,' I said.

'That's my line.'

'Don't leave me.'

'I wasn't going to.'

'I mean don't ever leave me.'
'I knew that's what you meant.'
'And — '
'And I wasn't going to.'

31 I've often wondered why I said that. It wasn't that I had any cause to regret it; not at least till many years after. It was simply so out of scale with all I knew about myself. I was a singularly even-paced man. I did little that surprised anyone else, let alone myself. It was such a wild move.

It seems to me now that I acted as I did out of desperation. I had behaved quite reasonably through all the alarms and traumas of Leila's defection; now the invisible emotional computer inside me was doing its silent work. I felt totally alone. I say this not in explanation but as a matter of stony fact.

For me, loneliness is the worst of all human travails. Perhaps, put like this, it sounds as if I wanted Jill only for the certain knowledge of a friendly hand in the dark. That would be a travesty of the truth. Yet it was undoubtedly the secret spring that precipitated me into that astonishing claim or bid or overture, call it what you like.

I did it for dozens of reasons, yet one over-riding all the rest. It was evident, first, that we had learned the same code. There was a private language at once established between us. With her, I was no longer an island, but part of the main. I was no longer aware of the terrifying loneliness that assails urban man in his weary voyages, the pain of isolation in long-distance jets, the stab of separateness in airports, the ache of solitariness in distant hotels; even humane and civilised ones like the New York Algonquin.

32 That evening at the Algonquin there was a big attraction on American TV: Part One of *The Godfather*. The networks had paid ten million dollars for it and to judge from the number of advertisements which interspersed the opening sequence, were determined to get their money back and then some. The Algonquin was quiet and I decided Brando would blend well with a bottle of Scotch and some nuts. I'd hardly settled in to the particular pleasure of watching that well-chiselled mug in action again when my telephone rang:

'Hello, Ben. This is Charles. How *are* you, buddy?'

'Charles! This is a surprise. What brings you to New York on a Saturday night when Brando is on the box?'

'Business, Ben. Business and pleasure. May I talk with you?'

'Of course. Where are you?'

'In the lobby.'

'Good grief. Come on up then.'

He was in my room a minute later; still in essence the same high-gloss product that had turned us all on in the roaring days at Oxford, but the body was a little heavier, the face more etched in. The flannel suits still came, I guessed, from the same tailor in the High Street, though custom-built tailoring was a luxury ninety-nine Englishmen in a hundred could no longer afford. He still had those bulging blue eyes which both mesmerised and alarmed, but tonight they were bloodshot; never a very attractive colour combination. Brown-eyed people look better bloodshot, a useless piece of genetic lore which riffled through my mind as I shook his dry, strong, politician's hand.

'Ben, you old rascal! Has nobody asked you out?'

'No. I'm relieved to tell you the truth. Especially since Brando's on the box.' But all the same, without bothering to ask, I turned it off and poured him some Scotch.

'Ah, thank you, Ben. When all's said and done, what greater

114

pleasure is there than this oleaginous amber unguent that glows and warms and neither bursts into tears nor sues you?'

'It can kill you if you fall for it too heavily.'

'Ah Ben — the same old moralist! Anyway, how are you? How's the translation racket?'

'It's all right, thanks.'

'And — er — Jill?' He was not so smashed as to have lost his foothold on that slippery ground.

'She's all right. The same.'

'Oh. So you're on your own in our lovable old city?'

'Yes. At least I was till you turned up.'

He threw back his head and laughed, showing his expensively capped incisors. He was a credit to the art and science of American dentistry. 'Ben,' he said, 'aren't you pleased to see me?'

'Delighted.' It was true. The way I felt that evening even Charles Harbinger was welcome.

He lay back in my armchair and crossed his long well-clad legs. I recalled that in our day that tailor had one man who specialised only in trousers, another to make your jacket. I wondered if it was still so. For the sort of money Charles would be able to pay, it probably was.

It occurred to me that this was not simply a social call. And almost simultaneously with this self-evident perception, it occurred to me too how slow I'd been to get that message. And then on top of these two insights came a third just as quick: a flood of relief that in my dry line of business, the examination of human motives was not paramount; though of course it came in. Anyway, it was not just a social call, as Charles now showed.

'Ben, I need your help.'

'Go ahead.'

'Have you heard from Leila? You know of course that she's in town?'

'Yes. She wrote me a note.'

'Yes, of course. After all, she's an old friend of yours.'

'Yes.'

We seemed to be covering the terrain with some difficulty, so I decided to speed things up a trifle.

'I'm seeing her tomorrow.'

But I was telling him what he already knew. He hardly seemed to take in what I had said.

'Of course. Ben, have the security people been on to you about her?'

I guessed that he knew the answer to that question, too.

'A rather curious Admiral called on me this morning and asked me some questions about her.'

'And about me?'

'And about you.'

'Uhuh.' He pondered this already given and processed information. 'And what did you say, Ben?'

'Not much.'

'Attaboy.'

'Of course it's always difficult with security people. One doesn't wish to appear totally unhelpful.'

'No, of course not. I have a good deal to do with them, and I'm all for trying to help.'

'Do you have to do with the Admiral's outfit?'

'You mean have my own boys turned against me? Not exactly. I have a general responsibility for surveillance in this area.'

I couldn't help reflecting on the sloppiness of official American English; the kind Charles was now using as a smokescreen. The English language is more cared for in America than anywhere else in the vast English-speaking comity; enormous sums are poured yearly into teaching it, ratifying it, using it, storing it. American English, the unfettered language, is a lusty young giant. American English, the sturdy growing tree, hisses with sap. American English, the delicious dish of mixed tongues, bubbles with the juice from a hundred varieties of argot. But official American English is a dollop of dough. Or, not to put too fine a point on it, official American English is a pain in the arse.

This was the kind of English Charles was now using.

'So you knew he'd been to see me?'

'Let's say I had an idea.'

'That's what we need more of. More ideas. Fewer facts.'

'Strange you should say that, Ben. Because that's the difference between your lot and my lot. I mean between America and Europe. You have the ideas, we have the facts.'

'Facts don't hurt. Ideas do.'

'Touché, Ben. You mean we shouldn't be ashamed of our honest bricks and mortar?'

'You needn't be ashamed at all.'

'A lot of us are.'

'Don't be — please. Forget it.'

'All right, Ben; I will. What did Leila say?'

'Not much. She just asked me to meet her tomorrow.'

'That's fair enough. After all — '

'We're old friends.'

'You're pulling my pisser, Ben, to use your own charming Anglo-Saxon vernacular.'

'Not very hard.'

He gulped greedily at the amber peace-giver.

'O.K. I'll level with you, Ben. I've seen her. I saw her the night she arrived. That was Thursday. I didn't try and hide it. I just called her hotel and asked her out to dinner. But of course they knew at once.'

'Line tapped?'

'Don't be so old-world, Ben. They don't need to do anything so crude with all the new technology. They probably know exactly what we're saying to each other right now, and you could search the whole historic fabric for a strand of wire.'

'They're eavesdropping through the green air.'

'Green air?'

'It's a gliding term. I've done a bit. It means rising air. Good air.'

'Clean air too?'

'If you like. You can't fly over smog.'

Suddenly he looked zonked out.

'Christ, we need some clear air in this God-awful city.'

'How was she?'

'She was fine.'

'The same?'

'To me, just the same.'

'Not older?'

'We're older by precisely the same amount between each encounter. Ever think of that, Ben?'

'Constantly.'

'So when you say was she older, of course she was older. But then, so was I.'

'Maybe you showed it less.'

'Maybe she did. Anyway, this is beside the point. Leila was the same. I'd changed, she hadn't.'

'You do yourself a disservice. Only fools and criminals never change.'

'Ah but Ben, a good slice of the articulate world thinks me both.'

'And a good slice, including all those whose opinion you value, think you nothing of the sort.'

'At any rate till last Thursday.'

'On such a little thing they could bend your good name?'

'The President's principal advisers do not normally socialise with the enemies of their country.'

That word socialise is a good example of what I mean by the dollop of American dough. It was not Charles's habitual style.

'I should have thought they do it all the time.'

'Not without good reason. Not without the President knowing. Not without anybody knowing. Not for *fun*, for Christ's sake.'

'What harm can she possibly do now?'

'She can do me all the harm in the world.'

He was thinking out loud.

'All you have to do is nothing.'

'You're naive, Ben. That's the civil servant in you coming out. You want to play it by the rule book. I've done nothing to be ashamed of so I've nothing to worry about.'

'If that's all there is to it.'

'Pour me another, would you, Ben old chap? Ah, that's better.'

'I suggest we leave the rest of this conversation to another day and another place.'

'No, let's consider the possibilities, Ben. Or as they say back home in Washington, let us assess the parameters of probability.'

'Have it your own way.'

'The first possibility and received idea is that Leila is herself a defector; a conspirator with Roscoe; an equal partner in treason.'

'I've always thought that was boloney.'

'So have I. A variant would be however that she was not so much a defector as a daughter of Mother Russia, a patriot who had never really turned her back on the land of her ancestors.'

'That's boloney, too.'

'O.K. A third variant would say that she was just a woman

who let her heart rule her head, who took off with Roscoe because she loved him. Have you noticed, Ben, how in every big defection case since the war, the wife has always followed her husband to the other side? No one credits a woman with placing ideology above emotion, country over lover, loyalty to a land over fidelity to a man. Did you notice that?'

'There must be exceptions, though I confess I can't think of them.'

'You can't because there aren't, Ben. Let's rule out, too, trivial motives like venal gain. Leila didn't need any material goal she hadn't well within her reach.'

'Just a minute. We haven't dismissed your previous motive yet.'

'Roscoe? You don't believe that, Ben, nor do I.'

'I think she may have felt sorry for him.'

'And for this she deserts the country that has saved her life and honoured her father? Not just because she felt sorry for him, Ben; that won't do.'

'Well, I still say she was sorry for him, but I agree that could hardly have been the reason in itself.'

'O.K. then. What are we left with? Some fit of pique? A temporary brainstorm? Some onset of undiagnosed paranoia?'

'Of course not. Leila was the sanest person I ever met.'

'All right then, young Ben.' He lay back in his chair, his long arms spread wide. 'What in hell's name did she go for?'

'I've often asked myself that question.'

'And you've never seen the solution that was staring you in the face?'

'No.'

Now through the fuddle of the booze he was grave as a piece of stone.

'It has occurred to me, Ben, and to other glittering intellects around me, that it was an elaborate double bluff. If so, she's the most brilliant operator we've seen in our generation.'

'A double agent?'

'Right.'

'But if she were, you would know.'

'Would we? Do you Limeys tell us everything, Ben?'

'I thought we did.'

'Not so, my trusting young friend. Not quite all. Every government has one last trick up its sleeve, some hidden reservoir of knowledge, some extreme contingency plans to meet extreme situations. You know, for instance, there's a Pentagon war game about a nuclear confrontation with Western Europe?'

'That's absurd.'

'*Credo quia absurdum est.* Believe it, Ben, because it exists. *It has to.* If I'd been sitting in this armchair three years ago, and shot you the Watergate scenario, wouldn't you have assumed that it was time the men in white coats came for your old buddy Harbinger?'

'I admit it would have sounded improbable.'

'Improbable! It's psychedelic! And yet in iced truth it actually happened.'

'You mean the British used her as a double agent without telling the Americans.'

'I didn't accuse the British. There are other allegedly friendly nations who are only too glad to take our dollars and spit on us when our back's turned.'

'Or is it possible that someone back there in Washington isn't telling you the whole story?'

'Ah!' His actorish face clouded over. '*Quel cinéma.* As I say, Ben, anything is possible.'

'That's why you took her out to dinner — to find out?'

'I was curious. I didn't expect for a minute that she'd tell me, but I reckoned I could guess. You get to have an instinct for these things in my line of business.'

'And did you?'

'Frankly no. We talked about old times, and a little about poor Roscoe, and a bit about her parents, and then — Goddammit, what do you think we talked about then?'

'No idea.'

'Children.'

'But she doesn't have any children.'

'Not hers, dope. Children, the generic class of '93. The new generation of children.'

'That's hardly surprising. After all, she is a distinguished paediatrician.'

'I know, Ben. But it was so — oblique. It was nothing to do with anything.'

'If you had children of your own you wouldn't say that.'

He remembered.

'I'm sorry, Ben. I'm particularly sorry to say that to you. But you see what I mean; it's as far from questions of loyalty as any subject can be. It's — totally uncontroversial.'

'Maybe that's why she took it up.'

'It doesn't explain why she did it. For Christ's sake, there are enough children to practise her skills on in the West.'

'So you were none the wiser.'

'No. So in the end I just asked her straight out. I said, Leila, why the hell did you do it?'

'And what did she say?'

His face showed his exasperation.

'She said: "Charles, why are you so unhappy?"'

'A good question.'

'Maybe; but no kind of goddam answer.'

'So —'

'So then she got up and kissed me fondly and said she had to dash back to her hotel because she had to prepare a paper on malnutrition for the next morning.'

'How frustrating for you.'

'You can say that again. But when I was thinking it over next day, I remembered that one theme did keep coming back again and again in our conversation.'

'Really? And what was that?'

'You, Ben. Good old Ben. She seemed more interested in hearing about you than in the innermost secrets of the White House.'

'What excellent taste she always had.'

'And that's when it occurred to me that she might tell you something she hadn't told me.'

'And if she did, I would no doubt pass it on.'

'Not in so many words, of course not, Ben. But you might be able to indicate some generalised area —'

'That comes within the responsibility of your surveillance?'

'Come on, Ben, you're doing it again and it doesn't suit you.'

'Doing what?'

'Pulling my pisser.'

'I wouldn't dream of such impertinent behaviour to a friendly power.'

'Will you remember what I said, Ben?'

'I don't see how I can forget.'

33 Leila's going seemed to remove the lynch pin from our little world. The two foreign scientists, Ed Ashburn and Harry Bahadur, had by this time already completed their apprenticeships with Sir Jakub and gone to glittering jobs in California. Daniel had stayed on in isolated, craggy splendour until the moment of his irrevocable decision. But once Leila had gone, the heart seemed to go out of the house. Her father accepted an offer to go to Jerusalem University, and the house was shut up, mournful and desolate again. My grandparents worked bravely on until it passed into the hands of an appalling man who had made a fortune from beefburgers. They worked for him for a while but their hearts were not in it. Our lives had in any event been diverging; now there were only duty visits to my grandparents to take me occasionally back there. And yet the influence of that house has never left me, and it still haunts my dreams. People were good to me after Leila went, as if I'd suffered a bereavement. There were three letters I especially treasured.

> Professor H. O. Bahadur,
> Nuclear Physics Center,
> Berkeley,
> California, U.S.A.

My dear Ben,

I was frightfully sorry to hear about Dan and Leila. He is a damned good scientist and we shall miss him though of course from the balance of deterrence criterion he may historically be proved right.

I am sure you are cut up about Leila. I have never told you what an absolute brick she is but maybe now I can. I should have liked her once for my sweetheart but she always resisted my amorous advances.

However she was fearfully helpful with some of my other adventures. I don't know if you still have that housemaid at Marston Mauditt, a nice healthy girl called Millicent Brownjohn. Well, you may remember she had a younger sister, Daisy, a very mature wench of fifteen with a superb bosom, what I call a real English rose.

Daisy was employed as a chambermaid at that charming local hostelry The Pitcher of Good Ale and soon we were madly in love. Unhappily my hot eastern blood prevailed over my usual caution in these matters, and I discovered to my horror that the girl was expecting my child. You may say this is no great facer to a chap of my proclivities and indeed it has happened before and since, but never with someone who is only just turned fifteen. Apparently you have some absurd rule in England about not impregnating virgins who are under sixteen, though as you know in my motherland that is considered the time of life when young ladies are at their luxuriant prime. It was a scrape for which I could have gone to clink.

Daisy told Milly who confided in Leila. She cleverly arranged for the two girls to spend a week's summer holiday with an auntie in Essex or somewhere. The fact was that during this absence the ill-timed impregnation was brought to a swift end in circumstances Daisy told me of utmost care and cleanliness. I at once offered to re-imburse Leila for the rather substantial fee that these things entail but she would take nothing. You will remember that she had begun to train as a doctor at Cambridge before she fell out with the authorities and she obviously knew the right people. In fact I should not be too surprised if she personally . . . but I simply don't know, Daisy would not divulge more.

I did offer to send Daisy to Tangier where there are some clever surgeons who can restore a maid's lost virginity but Leila told me not to be a bloody fool. She is a real thoroughbred, full of grit and fire.

How are you, my dear Ben? I do trust you will not let this unhappy business get you down. I hope to have a horse in the Grand National and if so shall certainly look you up in your lovely English countryside. God bless you.

Believe me, Yours ever,
Harry.

Dear Ben,

I felt I must write you at once about the tragedy. We both feel for you deeply and send you our sincere sympathy. Dan was a nice man but deeply disturbed and in great need of skilled therapy. The right analyst could have worked miracles for him. But it's too late for that now.

I can't help feeling Leila took advantage of his weakness. You know she had a very bad effect on all the scientists at Marston Mauditt. Even my dear Ed who is so steady and loyal fell somewhat under her influence. I always kept quiet about it before but maybe you should pass this on to the authorities for her dossier, it may help their reconstruction of her motivational processes.

You will recall my great fascination for your beautiful old English church brasses. I spent many happy hours in Hampshire on my knees making rubbings to illustrate my book which is still selling well here — *Knights and Wights of Old England* — did I ever send you a copy?

Anyway while I was absorbed in this wonderfully absorbing work and the children were safely tucked up with the baby sitter, Ed had suggested he carry out parallel research into old English inn signs for my next book *God Rest Ye Merry Gentlemen*. Ed set to work quite happily but it transpired that he got little further than The Pitcher of Good Ale where Leila used to go sometimes entirely on her own and drink beer with the local farmworkers. I need hardly tell you that this kind of behaviour has only one connotation in our country.

She soon began to interest Ed in the idea of joining the English scientists' trade union, I forget its name. I warned him about it but he became obsessed with the idea and went ahead. Now he is trying to start something similar out here at the Think Tank which has set his career back ten years.

She also encouraged him to talk about his most intimate personal hang-ups, the kind of thing people here only confide to their analysts. I'm not suggesting it went any further than that, it would be hardly physically possible because he used to come back from The Pitcher of Good Ale with the most wild erotic ideas and quite alarming erections. I grew quite worried, he'd always been so normal and steady before. Anyway, thank goodness, now we're back in the U.S. he's having analysis four days a week. It costs us a mighty mint of money, but I'm teaching school to help with the fees and you should see how those cynical spoiled Californian teenagers devour my talks on the Knights and Wights of Old England!

If this is any use, Ben, please pass it on to the right people, democracy is such a fragile flower and we who love it mus band together to fight for it.

Ed sends his best,

Your true friend,

Dot.

The Manor House,

Chipping Wroughton,

Glos.

Dearest Ben,

I'm spending the weekend here with Ronnie and his parents and we've just read that rubbish in the Sunday papers and I felt I must write at once and tell you not to worry about it. It's not so much inaccurate though I'm sure it's that too, it's so hysterically improbable that you could talk such banal balderdash. I'm deeply sorry I wasn't there to help you personally but as you know we're getting ready for the wedding which is going to be quite a big affair and I'd faithfully promised Ronnie's mother I'd be here for fittings and so on.

Daniel doesn't surprise me one little bit. The only mystery is that no one took the slightest notice — after all, he never made the least bit of effort to disguise his views. He may well be happier now insofar as he ever can be happy, I mean professionally anyway if not personally. God knows what would make him happy in that sense.

There is on the other hand something utterly baffling about Leila. It's nothing to do with her and Dan of that I'm sure. It's something else which we don't know anything about. You know I grew terribly fond of her. She was generous beyond belief and impulsive as only a Russian can be. Did you know that, last Christmas when I was first coming here to meet Ronnie's parents, I was scared stiff because believe it or not

on Christmas night they actually still dress for dinner. I had
nothing to wear and she came with me to London and helped
me choose a dress for that occasion which had that utter
simplicity you only get by spending an absolute fortune and
she lent me some fabulous jewellery, some Russian bracelets
and a fantastic necklace that is supposed to have belonged to
the Russian royal family. I can't tell you what it meant to
have someone like her to confide in and it made all the difference. Ronnie's people were absolutely charming and they
thought the dress super and I just wore this necklace and
nothing else which was a knockout.

I believe she still loves you, Ben, whatever her reason or
reasons for going and even if maybe she hasn't been absolutely
faithful to you in a narrow sexual sense does it matter a jot
and who is if you know what I mean. I can't write more
because Mrs. Brewster has come to fit the wedding dress
which is sensational. Ronnie sends his love

And so do I,

Sue.

34 ... And a man who could write that it was no disgrace to die in a public street showed not only remarkable prescience — for that is precisely what he did — but also a detached intelligence peculiarly and triumphantly French. Anglo-Saxon writers do not customarily die in the street and if they do they do not normally predict the nature of their quietus with such cool precision. It was almost as if Stendhal had planned it.

It was not a very brilliant essay — beta minus or maybe minus query minus. But it had one unquantifiable advantage. It was the last I had to write in the final modern languages honours schools. I laid down my pen and rubbed my eyes. We all know examinations count for nothing; still it was good to get it over. Degrees are like false teeth; you don't, if you've got any sense, flaunt the fact that you've got them, but you'd feel a bit of a twerp without them.

Jill was outside with the Triumph TR2. I yanked off my subfusc and jumped in beside her. She'd finished her last paper that morning. We kissed as she let in the clutch and in six or seven minutes were out in open country under a gracious English summer sky, heading west at seventy towards her parents' home in Wiltshire. First, though, we had to make a minor detour that we'd promised ourselves; to drink a bottle of champagne on the river bank outside The Rose Revived, the pub with the most beautiful name in England, though I think The Pitcher of Good Ale runs it a close second. It's at a tiny hamlet called Newbridge, so named because the bridge over the fledgling Thames there was new when it was built a thousand or so years ago.

They had iced it well.

'The last of the summer wine,' I said.

'I don't know,' said Jill. 'We've got about fourteen parties to go to before the end of term.'

'Yes, but I regard this as the last drink of my youth. Remember, I have to meet your parents in an hour.'

'They're probably doing just the same to stiffen their courage before meeting you, mate.'

'How could anybody be frightened of me?'

'How could anybody be frightened of them?'

The house was just below the Cotswolds, nestling in a fold of the hills, beside a meandering branch of the Avon. It was Jacobean; gabled, mullioned, made of pale gold stone worn smooth by the onslaught of three hundred English winters. It was the sort of house you see in New Yorker ads urging you to come to England, and indeed had been used for something of that sort. In the hall were the inevitable accoutrements of the English country upper-middle class: shooting sticks and silver-knobbed walking sticks and binoculars and very old check caps. Jill's father was smaller than I'd imagined and one of those professional nice chaps they breed in that part of the country. He was fiftyish and looked good for another thirty years. Jill's mother gave me that slight sense of shock all future mothers-in-law do if we did but admit it; she was a pretty accurate projection of how Jill would look in some thirty years: that is, like a charming watercolour slightly smudged by the rain.

If she was a snob she hid it pretty well.

'Do tell us about your parents, Ben,' she coaxed me over the Tio Pepe. 'Jill tells me they live in South Africa.'

'No, Rhodesia. My father's an accountant out there. Or at least he was. He's on the board of a number of mining companies now.'

'You've never been out there?'

'No.'

'And you live with your grandparents?'

'Yes. They've got a cottage on Sir Jakub Haven's estate at Marston Mauditt.'

'I know it,' said Jill's father. 'It's very well farmed.'

'We knew the Taverstocks slightly,' said Jill's mother.

'I'm afraid I was too young to know them well,' I said tactfully. And then with a sudden burst of recklessness: 'But I'm bound to say, though they know nothing about the land, the Havens have proved much better employers. For one thing, they've put in running water at the cottage, which we'd never had before.'

Mrs. Maysey took this in with no perceptible change of gear; but fortunately we got a breather.

'Ah,' said Jill's father. 'May I introduce my son Peter. Peter, this is Ben Freeman, an Oxford friend of Jill's.'

I had a momentary flashback to Uncle Matthew in *The Pursuit of Love* and his deep antipathy for what he called Oxford sewers. If Peter felt anything of that same ancestral loathing, he was an ace at concealing it. He was six feet tall, had hair almost as fair as his sister, and smelt faintly of Bay Rum.

'How d'ye do,' he said. 'Heard a lot about you from Jill. Can't all be true, mind you. No one can be that bloody perfect.'

'Peter, don't be rude,' said his mother. 'Drink your sherry and we'll go in to dinner.'

We arranged ourselves round an ancient oak table in the next room under a rather oppressive hunting picture. The family silver gleamed cheerfully as if to signify that in three hundred years of wars, taxes, and even socialist governments, nothing much had gone wrong for the Mayseys and, what was more, nothing much would.

'I thought I'd open some of the Latour,' said Jill's father as if suggesting we had a glass of Guinness. 'After all it's not every day that a child of mine takes an honours degree. I was quite happy with a shaky pass in agriculture.'

'And I didn't even do that,' Peter confessed, drinking his soup with the noisy confidence of an oldest son.

'He was a soldier instead,' his father explained.

'Oh,' I said politely, for he looked too young for the war. 'Where did you do your soldiering?'

'Windsor mainly,' Peter said off-handedly.

By such seemingly casual exchanges of code do the English upper class get their messages across. They were telling me in a roundabout way that Peter had been a Guards officer. On another occasion I heard one of Peter's friends say casually that during the Far-East war he'd helped build a railway. He might of course have meant a new siding at Clapham Junction, but anyone who knew the code would know that he meant he'd been a British prisoner-of-war employed by the Japanese on their notorious death railway in Burma. He would by definition have gone through God knows what horrors and would be lucky to be alive.

'How about you?' Peter asked.

'I was a soldier too.'

'Oh really? Which regiment?'

'I-corps.'

'Christ,' said Peter. 'Mind you, we could do with some men with brains in this family.'

'Don't mind him,' said Jill. 'It's mixing with the animals all day which gives him his elephantine sense of humour.'

Much later, when the parents had gone to bed and Jill had gone to have a bath, Peter asked me to have a whisky with him. Whatever his other defects he was a handy man with a jar, and poured out a noble measure.

'Tell me about this Leila Haven business,' he began without ceremony.

'What do you want to know?'

'Were you mixed up in it?'

'No. I was shattered when she . . . did that.'

'What do you do when you're not reading languages? Do you ride?'

'No.'

'Do you shoot?'

'I'm afraid not.' I thought it best not to mention the rabbits.

'Doesn't matter. Just wanted to see if we had anything in common.'

'It doesn't look like it.'

He stared solemnly into the log fire.

'This thing with you and Jill is a bit sudden, isn't it?'

'I suppose it is.'

'On the rebound as you might say?'

'She's been enormously kind. To tell you the truth I felt pretty lost and — threatened.'

'Of course, women do enjoy putting a chap straight and all that — makes them feel wanted.'

'I suppose so.'

'You sure you're O.K. now? Seen a doctor and all that?'

I was overtaken by a quick access of crimson rage.

'No, I've not seen a doctor. And I'll tell you something else. I'm not answering any more bloody questions. I've been interrogated by the security people and by the press and by the college and by my friends and I'm sick to death of it. Jill means an enormous amount to me and I want to marry her. But I don't want any of your money, if that's what you're worried about.

I'm quite capable of getting a job and so is she. We can look after ourselves and we've every intention of doing so.'

To my surprise he beamed broadly at that. 'Good. Let me explain. Jill nearly married an awful shit near here called Nigel Stedfast. I was at school with him and I can assure you he's a toad, but a rich toad with a title, so my mother liked him. Fortunately Jill got over that one, but then she met another shit called Parcourt, who was a French sadist, poof and Marxist if you can imagine such a thing. Anyway after he'd knocked her around a bit we managed to talk her out of it. So you can see why we're a bit sensitive. One shit is unfortunate, two is coincidence, but three in a row would suggest we'd run into an epidemic of dysentery.'

'I see.'

'However,' he concluded, getting up. 'I think you're all right. Have one more for the road.'

'Thanks.'

On this unlikely basis we built up a warm and sometimes riotous friendship which I'm glad to say continues to this day.

35 We were married in June 1951, just over a year after we first met. It was, by the standards of Jill's family, a quiet wedding; there were about fifty people there. My own contingent was pretty small: my grandparents, Sue and Ronnie, Oliver and Millie, and Toby, who was my best man. He wasn't exactly my favourite person, but he was my oldest friend — that is, my friend of longest standing — and he enjoyed that sort of thing, while Ronnie hated it. We had the ceremony at Shallerton church where the Mayseys had had a family pew since the year dot, and the reception was at the house. My parents didn't come over, but my father and mother had each sent me letters:

Salisbury

My dear Ben,

Your mother and I are delighted to hear of your imminent marriage. I have made some researches and found that the Maysey family are very solid people. I am enclosing a cheque for £100 which I trust will help with some of the essential expenses, though of course on these occasions it is the bride's parents who take the brunt of the cost.

I do wish you would both consider coming out here. The climate is grand, the business opportunities most attractive, labour is cheap and badly organised, and the tax situation compares very favourably with that in the old country. I cannot understand how you can put up with that ghastly government though I gather its days are thank God numbered.

If you would both like to come and make so to speak a feasibility study I should be glad to send you both your return air tickets. I fear there is little or no prospect of my returning home in the foreseeable future; for one thing my tax position in England is still a keen subject of interest to the Special Commissioners.

Your affect. father,
John Freeman.

On balance I preferred my mother's letter:

My dear Ben,
Your father and I were so pleased to hear about your engagement. Jill looks a very pretty girl from your photograph. You don't say very much about her parents. Are they nice? Where will you live? We do miss you very much but of course your father is adamant about not coming back to England. There is so much to recommend this beautiful country: the climate, the scenery, the shops, the sport, the social life and of course the excellent servant position.

We are sure you will both be much happier here and look forward to your coming out at least for a holiday. England sounds a nightmare from all we read and we can see no future for you there. Why don't you do as your father did and come to live in the sun? Do write soon and give us all your news. I do miss you so.

Your loving mother.

Then there was a letter from Sir Jakub Haven, written in that immaculate Austro-Hungarian calligraphy of his:

Hebrew University,
Jerusalem.

My dear Ben,
We were very interested to hear by a letter from Oliver of your engagement. You know Kitty and I are fond of you and hoped one day you might marry Leila. But now a year has gone since she disappeared, and we have reluctantly come round to the view that she means to stay on. This is a bitter blow to us both. Although one can never hope to understand another human being completely, it did seem to us that she was a sane, balanced person, and quite un-orientated to the alternative political system. Yet no other explanation now seems possible. I can neither understand nor forgive her action.

There is of course for my wife the hope that one day she will have a change of heart and come back to us. I do not share it, and we can hardly blame you if you consider Kitty's fragile hopes too slight to build your own life on.

I had put aside some money to give Leila on her marriage. As far as I am concerned she is now dead, and since you are the son I had hoped to have, I send it to you with my blessing.

Your affectionate friend,
Jakub Haven.

A postscript read simply: 'Blessings and love — Kitty.'

A cheque for £1000 was enclosed.

Toby looked well in his morning suit. His naval career had come to a premature end — there had been some difficulty over the examinations the Navy insist on nowadays — and he had become a trainee brewer. It was a career which seemed to suit him exactly. He had grown even more epicene and caddish as he had matured, and we had nothing in common except the accident of proximity in youth; but then many friendships are based on little more. In some opaque way I need him.

'You know, Ben,' he said as we drove together to Shallerton church in the back of the wedding car, 'I always thought you might marry Leila, in which case all that hou-ha might have been prevented.'

'It was never even discussed.'

'Still, it looked on the cards. What a bloody good thing you didn't, seeing that she turned out to be a red as I thought.'

'I daresay you're right.'

'And yet you know,' he mused, 'in some ways she was a good sport. Like the night of my twenty-first, when she saved my life.'

'How do you mean?'

'As good as, anyway. There I was, sick as a dog and puking my ring up at my own do. She took me down to that potting shed and really pulled me round.'

'How?'

'God knows. Black coffee, pills, salts, actually got me to throw up, you know, and then I felt much better. Stood me on my feet again and put me back in circulation, but did it so discreetly that the old people never cottoned on.'

'I know what you mean.'

134

'Anyway, Ben my boy,' he concluded avuncularly, 'you'll do much better with Jill. God knows what she sees in you.'

'I think she thinks I'm lost.'

'Well, I'm lost half the ruddy time but no one takes the remotest interest in me.'

'Brewers don't get lost. They get rich.'

'Well, no one can say it's the loot in your case can they, Ben? Ah, here we are. *Courage, mon enfant,* I've never lost a bridegroom yet.'

'There's always a first time.'

36 We went for our honeymoon to Portofino. At that time the only pollution anyone had noticed in the Mediterranean was the fine film of suntan oil which coated the water with its dark rainbow sheen. Just as Colman's are popularly supposed to have made a fortune from the mustard that's left on the plate, so Ambre Solaire must have made a bomb from the gallons of their unguent, only just so lovingly applied to so many glistening bodies, that is washed away by the uncaring sea. It was in those days a matter of curiosity rather than concern. The tune everyone was humming then was a trifle by Hoagy Carmichael about fingertips touching, which seemed appropriate; we drank Negronis and danced each night at Paraggi where there was a film set masquerading as a nightclub. There were no droves of package tour holidaymakers yet, but much worse, Farouk arrived one night with his new queen. His pockmarked bodyguards lined the walls while just across the floor from us he gobbled pasta, gulped Dom Perignon, and puffed at his Monte Cristo cigars. She looked bored, and we didn't blame her.

We came home in September and got to work on the cottage Jill's father had given us at Shallerton. It was rather older than his own house, and had the usual problems — dry rot, woodworm, and deathwatch beetle. Slowly we sorted them out. We uncovered the original beams and, excavating through layers of brick and rubble deposited over the centuries, uncovered the original inglenook. It was eight feet across and four feet high. We rewired the cottage throughout and painted all the woodwork white. We took up the flagstones, laid a damp course, and put them back again. We gradually tamed the garden, planted vegetables, started a new orchard filled with crisp apples, fat greengages, speckled pears, and black cherries. We had our own herbs; basil, rosemary, parsley and dill. We trained wisteria up the side of the house, and filled the crevices in the walls that lined the boundaries of our land with aubretia, so that it made a riot of purple in the spring.

The cottage became an anchorage wherever we travelled: Heidelberg to polish up my German, Dijon to tune up my French, Beirut to add Arabic, which struck me, rightly for once, as the best growth industry for an interpreter. Jill came with me whenever she could; we lived in Geneva and New York, did spells in São Paolo and Vienna, and shuttled between Cairo, Riad, Amman, and Damascus. Whenever nation spoke to nation, whether in hope or in anger, there had to be a few people like myself.

The interpreter's skill is a very ancient one. When Marco Polo walked across China he got a big hello from the mighty Kubla Khan because he had bothered to learn the Tartar language first. The dominant language of international diplomacy tends to linger after the power of its progenitor has waned; so Latin was used for all dealings between the European powers till the seventeenth century. Then the enormous achievements of France from the time of Louis Quatorze onwards made French the official language of diplomacy; Benjamin Franklin conducted all his missions to Louis XVI in French; and even when the Congress of Vienna met in 1815 to decide the fate of conquered France, they were still obliged to use the language of their defeated enemy. Then it was the turn of the Anglo-Saxons; Wilson and Lloyd George insisted that English should be an official language at the Versailles Peace Conference. But the big breakthrough came at the Nuremberg trials in 1945. Up till then, consecutive translation was used; if a lawyer spoke for an hour, it took a further hour to translate him. With the judges speaking English, French and Russian, and the accused speaking German, that was a recipe for spinning it out to the Greek Kalends. Then it dawned on people that the human brain was capable of virtually simultaneous translation, almost as you dub a film. An American colonel of French origin called Leon Dostert was the prime mover. So that's how the Nuremberg Trials were conducted, and the advantages in time and money were so obvious that the United Nations took up the system too.

An interpreter is not just a translator. He is concerned not simply with rendering the precise meaning of one language in another as a translator is, but with transmitting a whole set of ideas; to put it rather grandly, he tries to harmonise the philosophies of divergent cultures. Interpreters aren't infallible. When Krushchev went to the U.N. he was reported as saying he would bury us. It was a pretty chilling message. What he actually said was that communism, being a superior system, would last longer than capitalism and would attend its obsequies. What a balls-up! Not mine, I'm glad to say.

While I worked, Jill struggled to make a career as a writer. Watching her try to write sometimes made me believe her when she said it was just about the hardest work there was. I sometimes reflected on the prodigality of human endeavours; out of all those millions of words so agonisingly born, how often was there a sentence made that deserved to live?

As for her own words; well, she wrote scrupulously, and you would search in vain for a sloppy piece of syntax. She wrote elegantly, but then she was an elegant person. I admired the energy and seriousness of her early books but if, God forbid, she had been stillborn I don't think the world would have been deprived of a single thought that mattered. Her novels sold steadily to her three thousand admirers; they were well, if sparingly reviewed; I suppose she was one of the hundred best-regarded novelists in England. The only difficulty was that I had no compelling desire to read what she wrote. I made myself read her work because it mattered so much to her. But I could never tell her the truth about it because the truth was that it did not seem to me then to matter a lot whether she ever wrote another word or not. In this, mind, for my money, she was one of a very large and, some would say, distinguished band. Her novels had heroines called Candida to whom nothing much happened and men called Jules who struck me as pretentious twits. She never appeared to write from life or if she did it was a life that was hidden from me. Certainly I myself never seemed to appear in any of them; I was a twit, of course, but not that sort of twit; nor, it seemed to me, could my psychological processes ever have been dissected, like layers of an onion, with such reverent care; there weren't enough of them. I think she wrote those early books for herself.

When she turned to children's books, however, she at once found her true métier. Here she was no longer constrained by the tiresome armour of required fact and circumstance that invest a novel set in our own time and place. Her imagination could roam free. She invented a dream world and peopled it with a race of enchantingly fallible humanoid creatures who lived at an angle to reality. Soon she had a cabal of devotees and not long after that began to nudge fame. It was about this time that the trouble began.

My own drinking pattern was fairly harmless; you can't drink and interpret, so while at work I stuck to a Belgian lager which was very low on alcohol. I usually drank Scotch only when I took off in an aeroplane; a kind of unconscious deference to the gods of chance. I drank champagne only at weddings, claret, if offered it, at dinner parties, and martinis at barbecues. I'd only been drunk three times in life and each time, I'm sorry to say, for I cherish the rogues, in the company of Scotsmen. I hated being drunk, the nausea and remorse. The prospect of a hangover was for me a sufficient guarantee of moderation.

Leila had been the stereotype of a Russian drinker; that is, she had long periods of total abstinence and then much too much vodka; that frightening drink which suddenly brings down the iron gate of unconsciousness as if it were a guillotine. Jill, on the other hand, was a serious drinker who always seemed to have the whole thing together. She liked to drink neat whisky late at night when she was working and she smoked continuously during these creative bouts; she needed tuning up to a sort of cool tautness.

The first time I noticed anything wrong was the evening we'd been invited to her parents' house to have dinner and meet a leggy, restful girl called Hilary, Peter's future wife, in whom he was already much interested. All went well as the drinks circulated before dinner. Hilary was not at all overawed, and talked a lot. Jill, however, was unusually silent.

'Feeling all right?' I muttered during a natural break.

'Yes, fine. Could you get me another whisky?'

I brought it over.

'Splash of soda?'

'No thanks.'

She drank it straight down.

'Good Lord, that didn't take long.'

'Bring me another. Please.'

'You sure?'

'Yes.'

Reluctantly, and rather tardily, I brought it over. It suffered the same fate as the one before. Fortunately, at that moment dinner was announced. It was a somewhat harrowing meal as far as I was concerned, for Jill sank into a more and more comatose condition.

'Jill, darling, do you feel all right?' her mother asked anxiously.

'Perfectly,' she said indistinctly.

'Perhaps you've got this bug that's going around,' said Hilary helpfully. 'It laid me out for three days.'

'Why don't you take her home, Ben?' Peter suggested. 'Hilary will understand.'

'I'm all right,' Jill persisted; and stayed. But when she eventually tried to stand up, she swayed like a boxer who's soaked up too much punishment and is out on his feet. I managed to catch her as she fell.

'I'll get her to bed,' I told them, 'and give you a ring in the morning.'

Next day she seemed all right, except for a nutcracker of a headache. I brought her aspirins and black coffee.

'Thanks, Ben.' She drank. 'Christ, that's better.'

'Shall I take your temperature?'

'I haven't got a temperature. Just a hangover.'

'Are you sure? It seems so unlike you.'

'I just had too much Scotch.'

'You certainly put it away at a fearful rate of knots. What was it all in aid of?'

'Nothing.'

'If you drank like that for nothing, it's rather worrying.'

'Nothing much anyway.'

'What though?'

She hesitated. 'I keep getting these ludicrous waves of anxiety about the central heating.'

'The central — '

One of the things we had done to the cottage was to install central heating. It had been perishing cold for four hundred years, and we saw no reason why we should shiver like our rheumatic forebears. The inglenook was charming, but nine-tenths of the heat from it went up the chimney, which was no doubt why it had been slowly bricked up over the centuries. We loved to burn log fires there, but to provide a cheerful focus and fragrance to the room, not to heat it.

'I keep worrying about the dirt behind the radiators.'

'Whatever for? I doubt if they are dirty, knowing how spotless you keep the place; but even if they were — so what?'

She drank some more coffee.

'Give me a cigarette, will you, please?'

She drew at it hungrily. 'Thanks.'

I waited.

'Look, Ben, at the risk of sounding as if I'd gone round the twist, those radiators obsess me.'

'Well, if they do, we'll just have to get rid of them. Have underfloor heating or something.'

'That wouldn't help.

'Then — '

'It's just something I have to fight myself.'

She seemed in control after that for a bit, and I thought little more about it until I came back from a quick flip to Geneva a fortnight later, picked up my car at London Airport, and drove gratefully west two hours until Shallerton came in sight. It was a God-given English midsummer evening, musky and murmurous, and I was content to be home again.

The front door stood invitingly ajar, but no one seemed to be there. I went round the place calling Jill's name. In the kitchen saucepans simmered and the whole room seemed to throb slightly with the anticipation of pleasures to come. It was a room full of a woman's loving care; but there was no one in it. I went round every room again.

Finally I noticed that the back door was open. There was an old shed at right angles to the back of the cottage, in which we had installed a 500-gallon oil-tank for the central heating, and the actual works of the entire, self-indulgent process.

The door of the shed was open.

I tiptoed through, knowing in some primordial layer of my subconscious what I should find.

Jill was lying on the concrete floor of the shed, her head under the oil-tank. It stood on brick piles, about a foot from the ground.

'Hello,' I said.

There was no answer, but she moved very slightly.

'How's the central heating?' I enquired.

'I'm trying to find out,' she said.

It turned out later that she had been there an hour.

37 I'd known Miles Cordell slightly in the army, and always liked him. Many headshrinkers do little to dispel our innate prejudices about them. They confirm our fears that all psychiatrists are themselves in need of psychiatric help. Many of them, of course, will retort that we all are. Miles, on the other hand, was a psychiatrist who gave an instant impression of solidity and sanity; he looked what he was, a thoroughly decent clergyman's son who'd gone in for a bit of doctoring. The main attractions about him from our point of view were (a) we knew him; (b) we knew him not to be overtly off his head; (c) we knew that he was celebrated for middle-of-the-road views on psychiatry; was neither boringly reactionary nor wildly far out. In short, we hoped he could help Jill.

He put her into a private clinic and kept her under sedation for a week. Then he spent another week talking to her, and then he sent for me.

I felt a little like a delinquent boy summoned to see the headmaster. What in God's name had I done wrong?

'You've done nothing wrong,' said Miles. We relaxed in armchairs; he disapproved of desks. I looked at him anxiously. His face was lined certainly, but no more than mine. If listening all day and every day to the testimony of deeply psychotic people had taken its toll, he was remarkably adept at hiding it.

'However, we'll run through your side of it again. When did you notice this first?'

'About a month ago; the night we had dinner with her parents.'

'Yes, but there'd been no signs before that?'

'She sipped whisky when she wrote at night. Been doing it for years. Never seemed to have any effect.'

'No,' said Miles. 'I don't think for a moment it's a case of

142

alcoholism. That's merely an escape from the real cause. D'you ever hear anything from that Leila Haven girl that caused you all the trouble?'

'We get a New Year's card. And we send a Christmas card. But there's never more than twenty words on it. Just things she'd like us to know.'

'What sort of things?'

'Usually her work. But last time she did mention something else.'

'What was that?'

'Her marriage.'

'Oh really? To whom?'

'Roscoe. The chap she ran off with. Well, it was inevitable sooner or later I suppose.'

'How did it affect you?'

'Not at all. As I say, I was expecting it.'

'And how did Jill take it?'

'She seemed quite pleased. She knew Leila very slightly, or at any rate by sight. She thought, like me, that it was logical.'

'O.K. Now — had any illness at all?'

'Strong as an ox.'

'Sex life all right?'

'Fine. I mean, perhaps I shouldn't answer for both of us — '

'She agrees with you. So it's probably not that. And her work's going well?'

'Very well. Her third children's book has just won a big prize in America.'

'Mm. So you have no money worries?'

'Frankly, no. We live pretty simply, and as an international civil servant I'm well paid and have no income tax. We have no children — '

'Whose idea was that?'

'Both of us. Well, we'd like some children, but not just yet. We're both busy with our careers, and we've been moving round the world a lot. We thought we'd wait a while.'

'Mm. Well, it always seems to me a bloody impertinence to tell other people to have children. Let's see, how old are you?'

'Thirty.'

'And she — ' he consulted his notes — 'is twenty-seven. Well, that's no age. On the other hand — '

'Go on.'

'I wondered if it might just help. We have to face the fact that she has a serious psychotic problem there. Now she's an intensely highly-wrought person, indeed it's this finely-tuned imagination that's made her so successful. But she wouldn't be the first gifted writer or artist to go over the edge.'

'Virginia Woolf and all that. She's good, but she's not that bloody good.'

'No. Now we could try analysis. But I really wouldn't recommend that. At least not yet. And there are the various physiological remedies — '

'I don't want her to have them.'

'No, nor do I. Well, lobotomy is largely discounted now, and I regard ECT as very hit-and-miss.'

'Is that the shock treatment?'

'Yes. It's quite painless, but I think it's a crude therapy.'

'The idea gives me the creeps.'

'Right. So we might try a more homely remedy. A bouncing baby. First, it'll give her something to worry about apart from these fantastic plots of hers; and then the tremendous hormonal changes involved might just shake her out of the psychosis. She's young and perfectly healthy in a physical sense. Mind you, I'd keep a close eye on her all the time if you do decide to go ahead.'

'Have you put it to her?'

'Not directly. I'd much rather you did.'

She was sitting up in bed watching television absentmindedly and sewing at the same time. She looked a little pale, but otherwise perfectly all right. I felt a quick wave of some complex emotion pass through me; compassion, certainly, and a sense of sadness at the transience of all human life, and a wild urge to protect her from whatever the madness was that troubled her.

I kissed her and sat down on the bed.

'How are you?'

'Fine. Thank you for the flowers. Look how beautiful they are.'

'Miles thinks you're doing pretty well. In fact he's prepared to let you out at the end of the week.'

'I feel much better, though it may be the pills. What else did he say?'

'He thought we ought to have a baby.'

She put down her sewing and looked at me appraisingly, almost as if she were wondering for the first time if I were capable of such a thing.

144

'You know,' she said, 'that's just what I've been thinking.'

She came home that Sunday. In the evening we piled up the logs and drew the curtains and threw the cushions on the floor. We both felt curiously high, although we'd had nothing stronger than coffee, and we were shaking like beginners as we made love by the fire. I had the unreal sensation that I knew her then for the first time. I knew who she was and forgot who I was.

'Oh my God,' she suddenly said, 'I'm — '

And though it was only a lovers' conceit, we both reckoned afterwards that it was precisely at that moment that we conceived our child.

38 We called her Laura. I was away working in New York when she arrived, and was playing chess with a Russian interpreter called Boris Davidoff when the telegram was delivered. Boris was a great bear but a charming one, a sweet and sad man. I often wondered whether he didn't prefer the fleshpots of Manhattan to the rigours of Moscow, but if he did, he never let on.

'My dear Ben,' he said shaking my hand energetically 'this is wonderful news. We must have a vodka to celebrate.'

We adjourned the game and repaired to the bar. He bought two neat treble vodkas — he always claimed this was the minimum size to equal a Russian measure — and brought them over. We clinked glasses.

'Here's to Laura and Jill,' he said.

'Jill,' I said. 'And Laura.'

He came forward confidentially. 'And now, Ben, your troubles begin.'

'What troubles?'

'I speak from experience. At home I have three daughters. They rule their old man with a rod of iron.'

'Oh I see. Well, I've a little time yet before the reign of terror starts.'

'You know I'm only joking, Ben. Actually my three girls are a great source of joy to their old dad. Cheers.'

The trouble with Boris, as with most Russians, was that he was incapable of doing things by halves. Indeed, as I've suggested, trebles were more his mark. An hour later, when he brought the sixth to the table, I held the pale and seemingly innocuous liquid to the light.

'Something wrong with the milk of Mother Russia, Ben?'

'Not at all, Boris. It's just suddenly reminded me of someone I used to know.'

146

'Ah.' He stared solemnly into his drink. 'Vodka often does that.'

'She was a girl called Leila Haven.'

I watched him closely for an unguarded reaction, but if there was one I missed it. No Russian goes to a foreign capital, of course, not even as an interpreter, unless he is a dedicated member of the party. It was as well to remember that. As he didn't respond I added:

'No doubt you remember the case.'

He grimaced with the effort as he went through his highly-trained retrieval system. If he was acting, he had been well coached.

'Haven. Haven. Ah yes. She was the girl who came over to us some years ago. You must remember, Ben, that these events are far less celebrated in our country than in yours.'

'Did you ever meet her?'

'No. But I have friends who would know where she is.'

'Could you get a message to her?'

'That would depend, Ben, on what it is.'

'Of course. It would just be hello. Hello and love. That would be all right, wouldn't it, even in Mother Russia?'

'Ben, you are pulling my leg. Of course it's all right. But — ' he frowned.

'What's the difficulty?'

'In our society as you know, there are wheels within wheels. Forces and counter-forces. I wonder if she wouldn't think I had some ulterior motive; whether I was — ah — on the level.'

'There's one way,' I said. 'Which will at least prove you've really spoken to me. Give her this.'

I produced the ring from the pocket where I always carried it.

Boris examined it carefully. He was evidently intrigued.

'It looks like a Russian ring, Ben.'

'It is. And very old. It's hers. Well, she lent it to me. Give it to her and tell her about Laura. Give her — give her my love and tell her to write me a proper letter. She can do that, can't she?'

He seemed genuinely hurt. 'Of course, Ben. And you really entrust me with this lovely thing?'

'Yes. I trust you with it. Just as she trusted me with it.'

'All right, Ben. I'll do what I can.'

39 But no letter came from Leila; just a brief card congratulating us on Laura's arrival. And after that even the New Year cards stopped. On the other hand, as Boris had predicted, I was soon enthralled by the continuous pleasure of watching Laura grow. She was a bright child, though her early efforts at orthography left something to be desired. Wherever I went, she wrote to me, and her letters give in a convenient summary the graph of Jill's long struggle with the furies:

11 May 1962

Dear Daddy

We miss you. Wen will you come home? We saw your picture with Mr. Krooschov. He looked cros.

I went to see Mummy in hospiddle with granma. She was much beter.

Love from Laura

3 Nov 1964

Dear Daddy

How are you. Do you miss us. Is President Jonson nice? Mummy came home today and is feelin all rit.

Love from
Laura.

23 Jan 1966

Dear Daddy

Here is a new picture of us. Wen will you come home? Mummy says it is very bad of her but I like it. Dr. Cordell says she can come home next week but she must sleep a lot still. Wen will you come home?

Love from Laura.

4 May 1967

Dear Daddy,

Happy birthday from us both. We wish you were here. I did the drawing myself. Do you like it? Do you think in French or do you say it to yourself first in English? I promised to tell a girl at school.

Love from Laura.

16 February 1969

Dear Daddy,

Thank you for the money. I am spending it on books. Did I tell you I passed grade three in my piano? Mummy is much better and we are going to the sea this weekend.

Love from Laura.

23 June 1971

Dear Daddy,

Thanks a million for your last letter from New York. I was very interested in the negotiations because I was doing a project on the causes of the Vietnam War. The more you dig into it, the more thin our case there gets. We have no choice but to extricate ourselves. I've been to see Mummy; she had a bad spell but is now much more cheerful. We look forward very much to having you home in time for the summer holidays.

Love from Laura.

28 August 1972

Dear Daddy,

I thought you'd like my O-level results. They are not as good as I'd hoped but no one did well in Physics and Biology. I thought you'd be pleased about the French and of course the English . . . I had a long talk to Dr. Cordell today. He is very pleased with Mummy's progress. Do you know it's over a year now that she's been entirely free of trouble? That's almost a record. Uncle Peter's asked us all down to his new house at La Garde-le-Freinet. He didn't really want it, but Hilary bullied him into it. Do you know that enchanted place? It's sleepy and full of the scent of pines but you can get down to St. Trop in twenty minutes . . .

All my love, Laura.

Dearest Daddy,

I was so pleased to get your letter. It's about time you had a really long leave. You're always so busy that you never really enjoy these exotic foreign capitals. Some of my friends say Paris has been ruined, is all glassy and plastic and venal but to me it's still a magical place. Perhaps being with you will help Mummy, this last bout of depression has been such a disappointing setback. I look forward to joining you at La Garde as soon as this bloody course is over. The French on it are either fantastically nice or perfect shits — such an unpredictable yet indispensable race. Curiously enough, the Germans are all sweet, the Scandinavians deadly serious. There's one Italian I rather like, his name's Vincenzo and I'm sure you'll like him, too. Now do enjoy yourselves in Paris and write to me soon.

All my love as always,
Laura.

Laura was right; there was still something magical about Paris despite the skyscrapers behind the Arc de Triomphe and the Wimpy Bar in the Boulevard St Michel and the tinned Beaujolais. It was one of those autumnal days when the light is so delicately golden that you feel as if you're people in a picture by Monet. It seemed only natural therefore that after we'd had lunch at our usual place off the Boul Mich — not, of course, the Wimpy Bar, our own secret place — we should go to the Jeu de Paume for another foray into that shattering cornucopia of Impressionism. I find about half an hour is as much as I can take, it's so overwhelming, and one's own reactions are so comically naive. So that's the *Déjeuner sur l'herbe*, one reflects, and yet I've had it at home all these years. They are so magnificent, and so profuse in their magnificence, that they deny credibility. We wandered about spellbound, like young lovers seeing them for the first time instead of the twentieth, and then we walked across to the little café next to the Paris W. H. Smith's, where the Englishmen buy *The Times*, and we ordered a glass of wine each. Suddenly Jill said: 'Ben, I'm happy again,'

150

and I could see it was true. Then we kissed as we sat there for a full minute, paid our bill, jumped in a taxi, drove to the hotel, and made carefree love in a way we hadn't done for years, and I knew for certain, without the slightest expert knowledge to support me, that Jill had at last come out of that terrible tunnel. It was, like all the best miracles, as unexpected as it was inexplicable.

40 On reflection, I can see that the unvarnished accumulation of letters from Laura to myself may give the impression that I was always away when she and her mother needed me most. If so, I'm sorry, but it's only a trick of the dimension; I was there far more often than not when things went wrong. We had plenty of good times to compensate for the bad, and we grew close over the years in that benign place. Apart from the pleasure of watching Laura grow, we enjoyed entertaining, and because of the nature of my work, gave hospitality to people from many parts of the world. It always amazed me how people who were normally up-tight round the clock would unwind under the mollifying influence of the English countryside and gradually immerse themselves in the aspic of our life. The French would enjoy the local trout, the Germans lapped up the beer, the Americans liked everything, but were knocked out by two details that to us were unremarkable: the fact that we had lichen in the crevices of the stone walls, and the incontrovertible truth that our lanes twisted and turned, a phenomenon that some of them — from the West Coast — seemed never to have seen.

We saw little of Charles Harbinger in those years but we heard plenty. His first marriage, to a rich, clever girl from Bryn Mawr, ended in a disastrous blaze of publicity which spread even to the English papers. The only good consequence of the disaster was his son Jason, a preternaturally bright boy who came to England on a scholarship to Winchester, but who left at sixteen because he wanted to form his own pop group and lead them with his gifted guitar; he made some dazzling records whose talent even I could appreciate. Jason came to stay with us, bringing his guitar with him; a tall, gangling blond replica of his father but with the faun's eyes and shy smile of his mother. Last I heard of him, he was living in San Francisco and making a quarter of a million bucks a year with his music. But he was not speaking to his father, who had meanwhile married a second wife, the widow of an old war-time brother-officer, divorced her, and married an actress called Lola who took a header from their forty-second floor apartment one day when high on LSD. Since then Charles had kept what they call a low profile.

41 Jill and I drove south slowly, sometimes on the Autoroute du Soleil, sometimes not, and using the Michelin guide in the only way it should be employed — to find the places, as it so eloquently puts it, *agréables, très tranquilles, isolés*. The food even in the one-star places, even these days, generally looks after itself. We loitered through Avallon, Avignon, Aix, and eventually rolled up Peter's drive around noon six days after leaving Paris. We found him, surrounded by his spectacularly blonde wife and children, sitting by his pool sipping a pastis and deepening his already efficient tan. After the greetings and kissings and disgorgement of presents were completed, he remembered something:

'Ben, some appalling shit has been trying to contact you here. Kept on ringing. Sounds like a Yank. Name of Plum, I think.'

'Really? I don't think I know anyone called Plum.'

'*Madame Delaroque*,' bawled Peter from the pool in the general direction of the kitchen. '*Comment s'appelle-t-il, ce type affreux qui a téléphoné plusieurs fois pour mon beau-frère?*'

'*Il s'appelle Prune, M. Pierre*,' yelled the *femme de ménage*.

'There you are,' said Peter. 'Prune. French for plum.'

'I don't think I know anyone called Prune either,' I said.

'Don't you? Well, he says he knows you. Sounds as if he wants to sell you some insurance, though if so he's come a bloody long way to do it. If you like, I'll tell him to piss off next time he rings.'

'Rune,' I said suddenly. 'Philip Rune. Investigatory Reporter.'

'Oh, Christ,' said Jill. 'Not that again.'

It was as if the sun had gone in, though it had not.

'The hell with it,' said Peter. 'Let's have lunch.'

They made a barbecue and already the marvellously barbaric scent of charring meat was imprinted on the air. We ate, drank and gossiped in the sun until nearly four, then separated for a siesta. I'd hardly closed my eyes, my arms round Jill as usual, when Madame Delaroque knocked on the bedroom door.

'*Monsieur Freeman,*' she said softly, so as not to awake the others, '*Il y a encore Monsieur Prune au téléphone. Qu'est-ce que vous voulez que je lui dise?*

'*Un petit instant, Madame, je viens tout de suite.*'

I rolled wretchedly out of bed. Jill opened her eyes.

'Where are you going?'

'The phone. It's Rune.'

'Oh God, must you?'

'I'd better see what he wants.'

That dreadful stateless accent had not altered over the years.

'Hello there, Mr. Freeman. How are you these days?'

'Not too bad, thank you, Mr. Rune. How about you?'

'Things are pretty nice, thanks, Mr. Freeman. Gee, it's good to talk with you again.'

'What can I do for you, Mr. Rune?'

'Well lookit, Mr. Freeman, I sure do hesitate to intrude on your vacation — '

'Don't worry.'

'But I'm involved right here in St. Tropez on a film project and we figured you might be able to help us with the characterisation problem.'

'I'm an interpreter, not a writer.'

'Of course you are, Mr. Freeman. But you do have an area of special knowledge we could utilise.'

'What do you mean?'

'The film's about the Leila Haven case. You will of course recall my book on the subject.'

'I've got it, yes. But what can I tell you that you don't know already?'

'Why don't we meet, Mr. Freeman, and have a confidential talk around the area?'

'Where are you?'

'I'm at the Byblos. But I could be up in La Garde in twenty minutes.'

'No,' I said quickly. 'No. Don't do that. I'll come down.'

'Let's have a drink on the quay,' said Rune. 'Why not meet me at Senequiers, say around the cocktail hour?'

'When is the cocktail hour?'

'Say five p.m.'

'O.K.'

Jill had surfaced when I got back to our room.

'What the hell did Rune want?'

'He's working on a film about Leila and they want my help.'

'If it's anything like that illiterate crap he wrote in his book, you should have nothing to do with it.'

'Of course not. I just want to head him off from making any calls here. I'm meeting him at five. That's his cocktail hour. Back around six.'

'All right; but don't say anything. You know his genius for putting words through his electric mixer.'

'I'll be ultra-careful.'

I found Rune sitting in the front row at Senequiers glumly drinking an orangina and watching the young tits jiggle by. He was still wearing a dark blue blazer and for all I know it was the same one. The years at the doors of the creative furnace had dried his already desiccated features to the colour of a parking ticket. Otherwise, he was the same old Rune.

'Why, hello there, Mr. Freeman. It's so *good to see you.* How have you been all this time?'

'Pretty busy, Mr. Rune.'

'I know, I know. The years go by and we lose touch with our friends.'

'And enemies.'

His face creased as if he had been afflicted by a sudden onset of wind. Whether he was indeed wincing or just smiling I didn't know. He decided to try a different tack.

'Gee, Mr. Freeman, doesn't it make you feel real proud to see all those fine ships right here in the harbour flying the Union Jack? It certainly makes me feel good.'

'Frankly, I only wonder how they can still do it. They can't be paying our taxes. Anyway, why aren't you proud of all the ships flying the Stars and Stripes?'

Rune looked at me uncomprehendingly a moment. 'But didn't you know, Mr. Freeman? I'm English. As English as you are!'

'You could have fooled me. What part are you from?'

'Blackpool.'

'You're joking.'

'So help me. But I've done a lot of work stateside. That's where I got the accent.'

'Yes, I was wondering where it came from.'

'Another drink, Mr. Freeman?'

'No thanks, Mr. Rune. You have a motivational problem, I think you said?'

Another spasm of wind. Or maybe, on reflection, the poor devil had a duodenal ulcer.

'I sure do, Mr. Freeman. You see, I'm working on this script for Mr. Wurlitzer — '

'Mo Wurlitzer?'

'Sure. You know him?'

'No. But everyone's heard of Mo Wurlitzer.'

I had only just finished a piece in *Time Magazine* where they had typecast Wurlitzer as the ideal of the new style Hollywood producer.

He was the most successful entrepreneur of his generation, and though still only thirty-five had already made three pictures which had each grossed a hundred million dollars. It was rumoured in Beverly Hills that he could neither read nor write. The driving force behind him, said *Time*, was a formidable young woman called Annabel Abrahams who was his Girl Friday. Her shorthand speed and IQ were both said to nudge two hundred.

'Mo doesn't care for my script,' Rune confided suddenly. 'He says he needs it like a hole in the head. I've got escalator clauses there, Mr. Freeman, which, if I do it right, could make me half a million bucks. But no script, no dough.'

'Sounds rough.'

'It's not Mo. Of that I'm sure. Mo's a nice, easy, simple man. It's Miss Abrahams. She says my motivation theory for Leila just doesn't figure.'

'Remind me.'

'You remember, Mr. Freeman,' said Rune hopefully, 'I proved conclusively that Leila was a double agent — the most brilliant operator since the war.'

'Oh yes, I remember. But I didn't believe it.'

Rune's face crumpled in misery.

'All right then, Mr. Freeman. What is the real motivation?'

'Did you ever consider that there might have been no motivation at all — just a mindless caprice?'

Rune shook his head sadly.

'For this, Mr. Freeman, I get no half million bucks.'

'Well, I'm sorry, I can't help.' I got up to go.

'Just a minute, Mr. Freeman.' He detained me with his skinny arm. 'Miss Abrahams had one idea figured out which maybe you'd tell me your opinion of.'

'I must get back — they're expecting me.'

'Miss Abrahams believes we could get to Leila through the children,' Rune said half to himself, his arm still detaining me.

'What children?'

'The ones she looks after. You heard she became a fine children's doctor and she has this Institute now right outside Moscow. Our researchers say she's just been made an Academician for her work.'

'I didn't know that.' I sat down again.

'Miss Abrahams figures,' Rune went on, 'that this hospital is the main thing in Leila's life. Now what would such a place need? Money? Sure, but the Soviets look after all the money she needs. But knowledge is another thing. Now Miss Abrahams believes there are some doctors in the United States have an expertise in some areas of children's medicine they haven't cottoned on to out there yet. Some areas they're ahead of us, some they're behind. So Miss Abrahams figures maybe she could fix up some accord with the Soviets for exchange of doctors and skills.'

'Sounds a good idea.'

'Could you help us get the idea to her, Mr. Freeman?'

'I wish I could. But I haven't heard from her in years. You're more up to date than I am.' I reflected. 'Tell you what though. I have a friend in New York, a Russian called Boris Davidoff. He's very well connected. He could get a letter to her.'

'Gee, that would be great, Mr. Freeman. Can you introduce me to Mr. Davidoff?'

'I'm not due back in New York from sabbatical leave until November. But I could give you a letter of introduction explaining what it's all about. I think Boris could do that. He'd like the idea.'

'That would be perfectly swell, Mr. Freeman. Miss Abrahams has an intellect I truly admire.'

I admired it too, especially when I got the note from Leila at the Algonquin, suggesting we meet on Sunday at three on Pier 83.

42 She was there first and we kissed in that slightly embarrassed way old lovers do who have not met in many years. She was wearing dark glasses so it was a little hard to determine exactly how she looked; in any case that was hardly the point, indeed an impertinence. But the voice was the same, and when she spoke, she brought the old emotions flooding back, unwelcome in their exigence, yet comforting too as they touched the chords of lost delight.

She took off her dark glasses as we set sail and threw back her head and laughed. Then everything was all right between us, as if the years had never intervened, and I took her hand.

'My dear Ben,' was all she said.

She looked at me in that appraising way women do, as if she had the idea of buying me or mending my ways or maybe both, and as she looked at me I felt the guilt sluice through me; guilt at not having tried harder, at not having known her better, at not having given her more; the varieties of guilt we all find on the death of old friends; or at their re-birth. Then there was guilt again for my own ageing, and regret that I was no longer a boy in love with her for the first time. Then there was the marvellous sense of gratitude that she had bothered to love me, and then again, the waves of doubt at her leaving me.

'My dear Ben,' she said at last again. 'It's time I washed your hair.'

'Yes I know; I'm sorry. It's just that I'm so bloody busy with my work that I never get round to it.'

'An extremely light trim, just to shape those incipient curls. And then some of that French stuff I used to use. Two rinsings. A good hard rub with the towel, and then let it dry in front of the fire and brush it out.'

'I'd quite forgotten how you used to do that.'

'I hadn't.'

I studied her more closely now; with both curiosity and fear. She looked much better than she had when I last saw her; more fulfilled.

'You look,' I said, trying to control my voice, 'quite marvellous. I'd been looking forward to this so much and was sure it would be a hideous anti-climax. But it isn't. It's as if nothing had ever happened.'

She laughed again, and then said seriously, 'Nothing has.'

The boat was moving out into the Hudson River and heading south. Soon it would cut between Ellis Island and Battery Park, before turning east to begin its circle of Manhattan Island. There were about a hundred sightseers on board. They were all shapes and sizes and ages and races; all caught up in a common moment of revelation; all there to pay tribute to this concrete quintessence of modern Babylon. No one noticed us.

'Now,' she said, 'tell me about yourself. Tell me about Jill and Laura.'

'They're both fine. Laura is soon going in for a place at Oxford. Jill — well, she's had a lot of mental trouble, but thank God, she's a great deal better.'

'Yes, I know. I saw Sue yesterday. They told me Ronnie was doing a spell with the British delegation. She told me a lot.'

'Ah, if you've seen Sue, I need hardly bother . . . '

'Nonsense, my dear Ben. She had her own story to tell. I still haven't heard yours.'

I talked about Jill and Laura. We passed under the Verrazano-Narrows bridge and began to head north up the East River, with the city going by us on our left in a mescalin dream like an old diorama show.

At length she grew serious and said, 'I was so sorry to hear about your grandparents. But they were both full of years and, I'd guess, content.'

'Of course. My grandfather was felling a tree. He swung the axe and pitched over dead. A marvellous way to go. My grandmother went out to put up the washing six months later. Same thing.'

'If there is no other intelligence in the universe but ours,' said Leila, 'and I don't think there is, we can only conclude that the gods of chance are particularly kind.'

'I sometimes think that if we could understand the laws of chance we would understand a good deal more than we do.'

'And our old house? Is it true what Sue tells me? Some awful sausage man?'

'When your father and mother moved to Jerusalem, they made the cottage over to my grandparents, which was extremely generous of them. Oliver and Millie managed to get the tenancy of The Pitcher of Good Ale, which he'd been angling after for years. A lot of people came to look. We'd had the landed gentry, and then, with your parents, the itinerant intelligentsia; and then when Scatchard arrived we'd had the lot; we'd got the beefburger bourgeoisie.'

'Don't be so snobbish, Ben. As a good western liberal, you should welcome this shining exemplar of *poujadiste* society.'

'He was such a bloody bore. Fortunately, my grandparents had the cottage and enough of their own saved to be independent of him. It wasn't that he was a brick-faced oppressor like Taverstock: it was just that he wanted them to serve Campari and sodas on the lawn to his appalling business friends.'

'And what about Harry and Ed, Ben? Do you ever see them?'

'I see Harry regularly. He's always on the move; always bobbing up at international conferences. Harry is doing fine. Ed is not such a good story. He finally went stark, staring bonkers — '

'I'm not surprised, living with Dot.'

'And ran off with a campus dollie with A's in physics and sweet tits.'

'Good for Ed. What about Dot?'

'The psychiatrist's couch, four times a week.'

'Of course. Well, she'll be happy. Look at those beautiful boys.'

A Columbia racing eight swished past. I appraised them with the half-conscious recall of old skills. They went pretty well for a row of yobs in fancy dress.

It seemed to be my turn.

'How's Daniel?'

Her face was momentarily opaque; then she was herself again.

'Daniel has done great things. I really believe he's fulfilled in a way he could never have been in the West.'

'And — '

'And what about me?' She turned into the question like a

yacht in a high sea. 'Daniel and I bust up. He married a nice square Russian lady who understands the Quantum Theory as well as he does. But we're still friends. He drinks too much.'

We'd passed under Queensboro Bridge and the guide had pointed out Sinatra's pad high upon the East Side. We would soon be level with Harlem. I took the plunge.

'Leila, why did you go?'

She looked at me for what seemed time to go round Manhattan twice. Then she shrugged, and gave one of her old, resigned grins.

'Now he asks me,' she said.

'I couldn't ask you before.'

'I asked you to trust me.'

'I did. I do.'

'And to wait.'

'I did.'

'Not long enough.'

'I was lost.'

'So was I.'

She stared moodily at the incongruous artefact that was solidifying on our starboard bow; the familiar contours of the Yankee Stadium.

'My father had four brothers.'

'I remember.'

'The youngest was called Bruno. A lawyer. And a dedicated communist.'

'So you told me.'

'When my father decided we must leave Vienna there was little time left. I was at a girls' school in the Vorarlberg, around 600 miles to the west. Bruno was to come and get me by car, and take me to the Italian border, where my parents were waiting. But the night he was due to come, the Nazis found out where he was living. He was already pretty notorious to them. So he never made the rendezvous in the Vorarlberg.'

'What did your parents do?'

'Naturally, they were demented. But Bruno got a telephone message to them saying he'd faithfully guarantee my safe passage. Seyss-Inquart had already issued a warrant for my father's arrest. So with heavy hearts they crossed the border.'

'You never told me this before.'

'You never asked me. Bruno got to me in the end — before the Germans anyway had cottoned on to my existence. And then there followed the most extraordinary eighteen months of my life.'

'You were on the run?'

'We owed our lives to the Austrian communist party. I can't tell you the crazy things that happened to us. At one point, he was working as a porter at the main railway station in Vienna.'

'But he couldn't have been a very convincing porter.'

'Exactly. A woman came through the station one day and said to him: "You're no porter. Come with me." She hid us in a garden shed for six months. But we always had enough. People — some people anyway, enough people — were very kind.'

'So when did you get to England finally?'

'In 1940. Bruno smuggled me over the Swiss border with enough money to make the journey via Malta and Madrid. Then he went back into the underground.'

'I still don't follow — '

'Bruno was a natural leader. As a Jew and a communist, he was doubly wanted. Once, the Gestapo actually had him in a police station and his friends got him out with machine guns. That's how much they wanted him.'

'He sounds like quite a man.'

'Bruno?' She smiled at me. 'The most remarkable man I ever met. He was always my favourite uncle before the war. He was much younger you see, only in his early thirties, terribly intelligent and full of fun. He used to take me to the fleapit of a local cinema and we'd see all the latest American films. And he'd take me to the Prater and treat me to rides on all the roundabouts. And then he'd take me to Sachers and buy me hot chocolate. And once he went to England for a conference and brought me an English schoolboy's cap which was my proudest possession.'

'Did they catch him?'

'The Germans never caught him, no. But the Russians did.'

'I'm not with you.'

'During all that bloody chaos a number of Austrian communists who'd got into Russia planned with the Russian government that they'd be parachuted down into the Vienna woods and organise a rising against the Germans. The Russians cynically agreed and dropped hundreds of them. But there was no organization to support them. The Germans simply butchered the lot of them. It was a mindless massacre.'

'Well in war these things happen.'

'Sure they do.' We'd reached the northern tip of the island, and the guide was telling us how as a small boy in the 1900s, he'd been taken to see the Indians who still lived up there.

'Sure they do,' Leila repeated half to herself. 'But to people like Bruno who've pinned all their life and strength to an ideology of infinite power, it's a betrayal that can never be forgiven or forgotten. He lost most of his dearest friends that way. From that moment he hated Russia; yet logically enough, never gave up his communism.'

'Most people give them both up together.'

'Not Bruno. But you see, that was worse; the Russians have plenty of enemies; but this was one of the innermost faithful who'd turned against them for ever. They heard about Bruno, and they got him, just before the ceasefire. They got him into a lunatic asylum outside Moscow, and they pumped him full of dope. Owing to the low state of the art, then, however, they never taught him the sweet path of reason. They tried everything they knew, but he steadfastly went on hating them. He was a decided embarrassment, because his name was known throughout communist Europe, and respected. He was an awkward knoll in the smooth face of the monolith.'

'You tried to help?'

'Sure we tried to help. But my father was beating his head against a brick wall. Everyone he talked to had sudden amnesia about Bruno Haven; he was hot; much too hot for any faceless bureaucrat to handle. And then someone in Moscow had a bright idea.'

I waited.

'Bruno was becoming more trouble than he was worth. It was clear he was never going to come back into the ideological fold; he was too celebrated to be liquidated or sent to a work camp; but he could be exchanged.'

'Exchanged?'

'Yes. What the Russian government needed much more badly than Bruno at that time was a top young western physicist. They'd just lost Fuchs. Some brilliant but anonymous *apparatchik* in Moscow put two and two together. They already knew Daniel was a potential defector; but he had a blockage about letting down his dear old working-class family and friends. They knew we desperately wanted Bruno back. They tried my father, who showed them the door — '

'So he knew?'

'Of course he knew. In Central Europe, you play both ends against the middle or you don't survive. He knew, but he wouldn't help. Then they thought of me. Young, radical, with a good track record of rebellion against authority already to my credit, and a little debt of honour to settle.'

'Honour?'

'My life, stupid. Bruno had undoubtedly saved my life ten times over. And here was my chance to save his.'

'Christ, how simple it all looks when you see it like that.'

'There was nothing simple about it at the time. I was betraying my mother and father, I was encouraging one of the best young scientists in England to defect. Not, mind you, that he needed much persuasion, just a little screwing up to it. Then there were all the logistics; they contacted me first in The Pitcher of Good Ale and then of course again when we were in Finland together.'

'And that's when you told them to piss off. I speak enough Russian to know that.'

'Yes. They have no sense of finesse, these new wave secret agents. But, of course, we talked again next morning, while you were still asleep — '

'While I — '

'Yes, my dear guileless Ben, while you were out to the wide, full of love and wine and sleep. So you have nothing to reproach yourself with. Christ, what a lovely sunset.'

We were on the home stretch now, cruising past the Little Red Lighthouse and with Grant's Tomb drowned in the golden evening light. But I was unable to take it in just then.

'So what went wrong?'

'Daniel went wrong. Having got there, he had a fit of nonconformist remorse. Bitter self-recrimination; the sense of having betrayed his working-class roots. The letters from his father didn't help. So he went to ground and sulked. No Daniel, no Bruno. So I just had to wait and hope. I talked to him most days, without trying to push him too hard, and I got to know him well. He's a good man, slightly cracked, but worthwhile. Finally, we got him to work though it took eighteen months, and finally we got Bruno out and into Yugoslavia, a pure communist system without the superstructure of reaction and repression the Russians found necessary.'

'Why did you marry Daniel?'

'Because he needed me. Why did you marry Jill?'

'Because I needed her. And because I didn't understand.'

She laughed at this. 'We've made the full circle of the magic island. Here's Pier 83 coming up again. And now do you understand?'

43 We had dinner at the Top of the Sixes, a restaurant high over downtown New York. From our table we could see clear across the rhomboid forest of Manhattan. Its brutal planes and naked power were softened by the onset of night, and as its black rectangles were stencilled with a million windows of light it became heart-catchingly beautiful.

'And not a soul knows you're here?' I asked.

'The two governments fixed it up. I'm Mrs. Davidoff. No one noticed or cared at immigration. I have the two determined gentlemen you noticed at the pier today who've been detailed to look after my welfare. But it's been immensely rewarding. I've talked to all the people I wanted to meet and been to see the hospital where we're going to set up our joint programme. Indeed, thanks first to the manic persistence of your odd friend Rune, and then to the awesome influence of Harbinger, I'm going to sign the accord tomorrow for the Soviet government before I fly home.'

'They tell me you could be the first person in history to become a second-generation Nobel Prize-winner.'

She laughed. 'Do they? What nonsense. And yet, of course, there's only one reason in the world why I would wish it.'

'For your parents?'

'Yes. He'd be so pleased. And so would she. It would make up perhaps for the sin that dare not speak its name.'

'You mean you and Bruno?'

'Yes. That's what really finished him off.'

'Maybe he was just jealous.'

'Could be. But — I should have written.'

'Why didn't you?'

'Because I couldn't find the right words.'

'Yet you found them for me.'

'They were the wrong words. They didn't work. Remember?'

'It was almost as if you didn't — '

'Didn't what?'

'Didn't care enough.'

She smiled wryly into the Babylonian night outside our centrally heated pool of luxury high above Peter Minuit's island.

'That's not fair. Didn't know, if you like; not didn't care.'

'Do you know now?'

She considered a long time.

'I genuinely believe I've done something serious with my talents and contributed something solid to human knowledge; even saved the lives of many young children and shielded them from unneccessary suffering.'

'You make it sound like a summing up.'

'It is. It's the logical end of the journey. This new treaty we're signing tomorrow is for me a living and symbolic thing. It's to do with life and healing, not power and death.'

'You could still be enormously useful. Your most important work could be in front of you.'

'It could be, but it isn't. I know that. Not the truly original work — the breakthrough that's dictated to you by the gods when you're dreaming at your desk, exhausted by the struggle.'

'Then — since you've given so much — wouldn't it be a good moment to start to think about yourself?'

She smiled.

'I once quoted a line of poetry at you, Ben. It asked who could be happy in modern Russia.'

'Haven't you been happy?'

'I've been fulfilled as a doctor. Not happy as a woman.'

'Isn't it a good place to be happy?'

She stared into her glass.

'It's a grievous place. Oh, I concede that millions of simple people have done better and gone to school and got their two-room flats and their hundred roubles a month and I don't despise that. Honestly I don't. And remember I've been a member of the *nomenklatura* — the Russian self-appointed aristocracy. But that never made up for the death of the will, the end of liberty, the abnegation of those necessary luxuries like doubt and dissent.'

'So — '

'So I got it all wrong. I thought I could save Bruno and thank heaven I was right. Then I thought I could help Daniel and I honestly believe I did that vital year and a half. I thought you could get on all right without me. For a while, anyway.'

'And did I?'

She put her hand on mine. 'Shouldn't you tell me that Ben?'

I thought it over.

'I've been very fortunate. Most of the time, anyway.'

'And the rest?'

I hesitated.

'May I flatter you with the truth?'

'I expect nothing less.'

'There was only one thing that still hurts. We wanted a son very much. We were expecting another child. But something went badly wrong and they had to end it. The doctor told her — and I've never forgotten or forgiven — that it was a boy.'

She frowned. 'That's why the work I've been doing has been so infinitely precious and worthwhile. But I'm sorry Ben, I didn't know that.'

'No one has known, except Charles, until tonight.'

'But you see what you're saying Ben? If you'd had the boy, you'd have been complete.'

'You have to take the throw of the dice. I'd lost you and made the best life I could.'

'But you hadn't lost me.'

'Now you tell me.'

'It's hardly seemed any time at all.'

'No; and yet — long enough to make it too late.'

She shivered. 'Those two awful words.'

'I'm sorry. They're also extremely arrogant. Who are we to say anything is too late? Sometimes the dice fall in our favour.'

'Give me an example, and I'll believe you.'

'What a happy coincidence that we should be here at the same time.'

She smiled. 'Dear naïve Ben. It was no coincidence. Rune told me when you'd be here. And I've helped him all I can.'

'Of course. How stupid of me. And where have they hidden you? Not at the Waldorf Astoria, I assume?'

'They've put me in an apartment that looks over the East River. It's full of Utrillos and Amerindian sculptures and they'd stocked the refrigerator and left a thousand discs in the hi-fi. But come and see for yourself.'

We sat taking in the view of the East River and sipping the VSOP brandy the U.S. government had so thoughtfully provided.

A little before dawn she said: 'I suppose those two rugged gentlemen down below wouldn't mind if you stayed.'

A little later she said: 'Oh Ben, I've missed you. Oh Ben.'

O night, O trembling night. O day, O gradual day. In the uncurtained day her naked love, my great good news.

As dawn came up over the East River she said: 'I must go and sign the accord.'

'And then you really have to leave?'

'Yes.'

'We can meet again.'

'Can we, Ben?'

44 Lunch with Sue Carter — or Mrs. Ronald Townsend, as she was billed in the society columns — that day at the Four Seasons was a handy piece of therapy; not that she was deceived.

'What have you been up to?' she enquired suspiciously. 'You look zonked out.'

'Arafat's in town. I'm extremely busy.'

'You've seen Leila?'

'Yes. We went for a boat trip yesterday. How did you find her?'

'The same. What an astonishing story.'

'Indeed.'

'Do you know what conclusion I came to?'

'No idea.'

'Only one person behaved really badly in the whole tangled business. Daniel did what his conscience dictated. Sir Jakub and Lady Haven did everything they thought they could. Harry and Ed remained absolutely true to themselves. Even Harbinger did what he thought was right and it's through his influence that Leila at last has her heart's desire. Professionally at any rate. There's only one true traitor.'

'Who?'

'You.'

'Me?'

'Yes, you, you bastard.'

'Why?'

'Why didn't you wait?'

'I was lost.'

'You just gave up. Listen, Ben, you know bloody well you never really gave up trusting her. Or loving her.'

'I've never stopped to work out exactly what I felt.'
'You just took the easy way out.'
'It hasn't proved all that easy.'
'You think it's been easy for her?'

45 'No, sir, it has not been easy. Not easy at all. It has been a most delicate business.'

The Admiral sat in the Blue Bar, half in shadow. He seemed somehow more human with a tumbler of Scotch on the rocks in his hand. He stared into it solemnly.

'It is never pleasant to have to maintain surveillance when one of the President's closest advisers is involved.'

'You know they had dinner on Thursday?'

He looked at me in surprise at the naïvety of my question.

'Why, sure we knew, sir, and there was Friday, too.'

'Friday?'

'That's right, sir. After they'd been up to Massachusetts to see the new hospital, they checked in at a motel.'

'You know what I say to that, Admiral?'

'No, sir.'

'So bloody what.'

'For anybody else, sir, I concur. So bloody what. But with Mr. Harbinger, so bloody something.'

'She's entirely harmless.'

'She told you about Bruno?'

'How the devil did you know about that?'

The Admiral smiled wearily. 'We have our methodology, sir. A lot of information comes to us from the other side of the ideological wall. Some we buy, some we overhear, some just drops in our laps.'

'Well, if you know about Bruno, you know she's harmless.'

The Admiral looked straight at me.

'Did she tell you they were lovers?'

'No. But in view of everything they went through together, it's hardly surprising.'

'You will recall her age at the time they were together?'

'Fourteen. To which I say again to you, Admiral — '

'So what. Mr. Freeman, you misjudge us. We have read Nabokov and we are neither shocked nor surprised. But we are deeply concerned about Harbinger.' Suddenly he was no longer bantering.

'Mr. Freeman, my department believes we simply cannot have a man of Mr. Harbinger's instability that close to the President. He is a most gifted and brilliant man. But he has no — ah, as we used to say in Latin class — no *gravitas*. He is simply not fit to be trusted with the terrible burdens of state he at present bears. And make no mistake, Mr. Freeman, we shall relieve him of those burdens sooner or later.'

'I'll watch the papers. And now, Admiral, if you'll excuse me, I have to get to the airport. It's been a pleasure to meet you.'

'You too, sir. Have a good trip. Come back to see us soon.'

46 I always caught the midnight Jumbo. For one thing, darkness hid that dire spin through the cemeteries of New York, for another, the improbable Leviathan lumbered east into the dawn and a new day and one saw the coast of England coming up in the early sunlight. It made the heart lift as once, ironically, the hearts of the English settlers must have lifted as they made landfall sailing west.

We had a sub-standard Barbra Streisand movie and a warmed-over steak and I listened a while on the headphones to some tinned jazz. Then I slept and when I awoke a magnificent blood-orange sun was spilling out its heart over the candlewick cumulus ten thousand feet down. Someone once said we interpreters were ham actors at perpetual first nights. In the same way, I reflected, the sun is a ham at unending first nights and infinite matinées. One day it simulates Armageddon, another Apocalypse; one day, a Technicolor, multi-dimensional trip; the next, in silent slow-motion, the nuclear holocaust. It was that unimaginable option my good friends had given the quick of their lives to provide.

I thought of the dawn coming up on the East River, and of Leila in my arms, not knowing then that she had left me a note in the silent apartment; the last she would ever write to me, or to anyone else for that matter.

80